BACK AT YOU

An Alex Troutt Thriller

Book 9

By
John W. Mefford

BACK AT YOU
Copyright © 2018 by John W. Mefford
All rights reserved.

Second Edition

This is a work of fiction. The events and characters described herein are imaginary and are not intended to refer to specific places or living persons. The opinions expressed in this manuscript are solely the opinions of the author and do not represent the opinions or thoughts of the publisher. The author has represented and warranted full ownership and/or legal right to publish all the materials in this book.

This book may not be reproduced, transmitted, or stored in whole or in part by any means, including graphic, electronic, or mechanical without the express written consent of the publisher, except in the case of brief quotations embodied in critical articles and reviews.

Sugar Hill Publishing

ISBN-13: 978-1709176-90-6
Interior book design by
Bob Houston eBook Formatting

To stay updated on John's latest releases, visit:
JohnWMefford.com

One

Alex

The words were like a hundred daggers, each one piercing a different organ, severing major arteries. Oxygen was in short supply. The room spun, and I reached out for the chair.

I blinked once, then clenched my jaw. Little sleep last night and hardly a thing to eat all day. Maybe everything I'd just heard had been a weird hallucination—had I been slipped a mind-altering drug?

"You must acknowledge that you understand my directions."

The digitally altered voice, sounding like a baritone haunted robot, stabbed me in the heart. It was no hallucination. And the person on the other end of the phone was anything but robotic. He—or at least I thought it was a male—had threatened me with the most terrifying weapon a mother could ever face.

Erin, my sweet, precious daughter. Please...if any entity in the universe is listening, help me...help her.

I could hear my breath quivering into the receiver, and I released an audible gasp, as if I'd just cracked the surface after being held under water. "Yes, I heard you." Another sharp intake of air. "I will do as you said. But you must promise me...*please* promise me that you nor anyone else will touch her."

Silence. I glanced at my phone. Was the fucking line still connected? I saw the time of the call, now showing 1:33 and counting. "Hello!"

"I am here. I don't like demands."

Too fucking bad, I thought but dared not say.

"You want me to pay this two-million-dollar ransom. How do I know you won't…?" A swell of emotion nearly rocked me off my feet. I bit into the side of my cheek, and the emotional tide subsided somewhat. "How do I know you won't harm her, or that she'll even be there once I get you the two million dollars?"

"You don't."

I was looking for some way of guaranteeing Erin's safety—and that of her friend, Becca. I'd talked to Becca's mom just last night when I couldn't get Erin on her cell phone. Becca's family had taken Erin along with them on their spring-break trip to Las Vegas. The mom didn't seem worried, said she was having a "tough time tracking down the girls," guessing that their cell phones had died or they were in a bad spot for reception or they were busy shopping at the Venetian. Her mood was light, though—nothing to worry about. She promised to have Erin call as soon as the girls returned. No phone call, so I let it go and went to sleep.

It was almost noon the next day. Brad, my boyfriend of over two years, and I had just finished looking at homes with a real-estate agent. We'd finally made the call that he would ditch his place and we'd buy a new home together, formally bringing him into the family that included Luke, my sassy thirteen-year-old, Ezzy, my equally sassy nanny, and of course, Erin, my independent sixteen-year-old.

"Look, I'll do anything to ensure the safety of my daughter, and her friend too. Anything. But I don't have two million dollars. Give me a few days, and I'll see what I can do. Or I can wire you some money...maybe ten grand, and then promise to pay you another ten grand if you release Erin and Becca."

A pause. This one longer than the last. I gritted my teeth, waiting for a signal. If they'd done any research at all, they had to know that I didn't have access to two million dollars, today or even if we waited a month. Maybe they were desperate for money. To someone grasping to the edge of the mental cliff, ten grand might make them jump at the offer.

"You have not been listening to me." Agitated.

"No, it's just that I'm being honest with you. You want me to be honest, right? I don't have two million dollars. I don't know anyone who has that kind of money. But I can get you ten grand. Like I said, I'll even wire it to you now...if I know you'll drop the girls off at the police station. Once I have validation they're okay, I'll send you the other ten grand. I promise."

I knew it sounded lame the moment I'd said it. *I promise?* Was I fucking delirious, thinking this was some dispute with the president of the neighborhood homeowner's association?

"I thought you cared about your daughter, Alex."

"I do. Believe me, I care. She's my world. Don't hurt her...please," I said with a sniffle. I didn't sound like a seasoned FBI agent. Almost everything I'd learned had seemingly been sucked from my mind.

"If you care, then you'll follow the instructions."

"I don't have two million dollars, though. Are you hearing me?"

"Are you fucking hearing me, Alex Troutt? You don't question my methods. You're not allowed to ask if I will hurt your daughter. You will follow my instructions, or she and her friend will both die. And it will not be a quick death, that I assure you."

"Okay, okay...please, just..." I stopped myself from asking.

It would do no good.

"You have eight hours to get to the Vegas airport. Once there, I will text you further instructions. Again, I must stress that you do not tell anyone. Not a soul. I know you work for the FBI. You probably believe they can help you. They can't. If you contact them, we will know. And we will kill Erin and her friend. Is that understood?"

"Yes."

The line went dead.

My chin dropped to my chest. Brad walked into the living room.

"Dear God, Alex! What's wrong, babe?" He wrapped an arm around my quaking shoulder.

I lifted my tear-filled eyes and opened my mouth. Before I could say a word, the phone vibrated in my hand.

Were they calling again?

Two

I punched the green button on the phone before I looked at the number. "Did you decide you'd rather have the ten grand?"

"What the fuck is going on, Alex?"

My brain did a double-take. It was Sonya Faulk, Becca's mother.

"Sonya, what do you know?" I held the phone away from my ear so Brad could listen. I had to share this horror with him, if no one else.

"I just know that I received…" She gasped out a few sobs, then a grunt, as if she had to clip the emotion off before it took hold of her. "I received a call from a man…or woman, I'm not sure. They have our daughters, Alex. These monsters have our daughters!"

She'd received a ransom call too. Brad squeezed my shoulder, his eyes wide with distress. I gave him a quick nod and tried not to hyperventilate.

"Sonya, I received the same call. Please tell me what—"

"What have you done for them to take our daughters, Alex? You've got to tell me. This can't be. This can't be." She began to sob. And then I heard some shuffling.

"Sonya, we have to keep—" I started.

"I'm not going to sit around and take orders from some

woman." It was the dad, Byron, and his anger was off the charts.

"Byron, I was telling Sonya that I received the same call. We're in the same situation. But I need for you to tell me what they told her…or you. Who received the call exactly?"

"Dear God, Alex, what in the hell have you done now?" He wheezed as he inhaled, sounding as though he'd lost a lung.

Another glance at Brad. The pain etched on his face was another reminder of how very real this situation was.

"Byron, it's not about me." I paused a second, instantly questioning whether my FBI life had invaded my personal life. Didn't matter, not now anyway. "Just please tell me what they told you or Sonya."

"I got the call," Sonya said, her phone apparently now on speaker.

"Just in the last few minutes?"

"Yes, yes. Just tell us what's going on, Alex," Sonya continued. "We have to get our Becca back. She's our only child. We don't have another one like you do."

I shook my head at the suggestion that my kids were any less important just because I had more than one. How could she say such a thing? I bit back a snarky comment.

"Sonya, Byron, please listen for a second. I received the same call. I hung up with them just seconds before you called. Please tell me what they told you."

"I'm not sure we can trust you. You're involved in something seedy. I know it. Can't trust the FBI worth a shit these days."

Byron wasn't helping our situation with his vitriol. And I knew I had to get to the airport. Hell, this call could very well be monitored somehow.

I lost it. "Byron, shut the fuck up! This isn't helping. You want to get our daughters back, then I need you to answer my questions."

A couple of seconds of silence. Brad nodded his approval of my tactic. I put a hand on his shoulder now, my knees wobbly.

"Okay, okay," Byron said, his defenses suddenly lowered. "I didn't hear the beginning of the call. Sonya?"

I heard some sniffling. "They had a freaky voice. It was disguised in some way."

I nodded at Brad and pointed at myself—he returned the nod, indicating he understood that I, too, had heard a similar voice.

"And what did they say?"

"That they had our Becca and her friend, Erin. And that we should not go to the police or any law enforcement to tell them of their disappearance. If we did, then they would…" She couldn't say the words out loud. My heart ached, and tears welled in my eyes. I wiped my face.

"What else, Sonya?"

"Just that they would turn over the girls once Alex Troutt completed a task for them."

A task? I hadn't been charged with any task. Just a money demand. I gnawed on the inside of my cheek.

"What is this task, Alex? That's why we called. That's why Byron is so mad. I'm mad…upset. I know you wouldn't do anything to purposely harm our Becca, would you?"

"What? No. So, did they ask you for a ransom?"

"Actually, I asked them if they wanted money, and they just said that they knew we couldn't afford it, and if we wanted to see our daughter alive, we had to wait for you to complete this task. I know we're taking a chance by calling you, but we couldn't just sit here in our hotel room and do nothing."

"I understand. Sonya, Byron, listen to me for a second. I've done nothing to get our daughters in trouble. The kidnappers called me and told me I had to give them two million dollars. They knew I didn't have the money, so they told me I'd get further instructions once I landed at the Vegas airport."

"But why you? Why didn't they ask us to do this task? We're already out here," Sonya said through sobs.

"I don't know, Sonya. I'm trying to figure this out as we're talking. It's not making much sense."

I asked where they last knew the location of Erin and Becca.

"Shopping at the Venetian," Sonya said. "That's a high-end hotel-casino. They're sixteen years old. It was early evening. Shouldn't be any problem. Security is all around. Byron and I were catching a show to see Mariah Carey."

The Venetian. I wondered if the kidnappers had somehow lured the girls to a room in the hotel.

"Okay, I need to get to Logan airport. I'll try to be in touch as much as I can, once I hear back. Brad is here. If you can't reach me, you can try him. I'll have him text you his number."

"Alex..." It was Byron again, his throat scratchy. "I'll do anything to get my Becca back. So, I didn't mean to accuse you of anything. Just do whatever it takes."

We were finally on the same page. Whatever it took, I would bring Erin and Becca home.

Three

The Las Vegas sun couldn't be the same as the one above Boston. Or maybe Vegas was about a thousand miles closer to the sun. That had to be the case. Or something like that.

One step outside the doors of McCarran International Airport, and the sun's rays hit me like a weaponized laser beam. I cupped my hands over my eyes—I'd forgotten my sunglasses—and all I saw was flat land and cookie-cutter homes. When the plane had descended onto the runway, I'd seen the other side of Vegas, the glitz-and-glamour side, the one that sparkled like diamonds at night, where oddly shaped buildings looked like foreign objects with the Spring Mountains hulking in the background.

I glanced at my phone. I had four bars, so the signal was good. But I hadn't received any text messages or phone calls. During the first half of the four-hour flight, I was tighter than the strings on my old tennis racket. I even considered taking up the flight attendant's offer for one of those tiny bottles of tequila—well, actually about three of them. But I declined, not wanting to sacrifice my mental acuity just to minimize my stress level.

After closing my eyes and doing some deep-breathing exercises, I finally relaxed enough to think semi-clearly. I replayed the kidnapper's call at least fifty times in my mind, hoping to remember something that I hadn't caught during the actual event. Every time, though, the replay was the same. My brain was either still in shock or the details had simply dispersed like untethered molecules. Nothing new came to me, and by the time the wheels screeched against the Las Vegas runway, I felt quite agitated with myself.

Another glance at my phone. No activity. All I saw were my white knuckles grasping the phone. Yep, I could feel my tension surging back into the red zone.

Damn, I wish someone was with me. Brad was a gentle soul, a real saving grace for my life. Before walking out of the house, I'd given him the complete rundown on my call with Darth Vader, just providing the facts, trying to still my emotions, so that he'd know what was going on. We agreed that, for now, he'd tell Luke and Ezzy that I was ordered out of town on urgent FBI business. To them, that was almost normal. Brad kissed me, gave me a quick hug, and said to keep him in the loop.

Brad was one of the best intelligence analysts in the FBI. He was also twelve years my junior. After some disconcertion about being "that woman," the cougar, I'd embraced having a hunk on my arm. But right now, I needed a badass partner, someone who wasn't as consumed as I was with the kidnapping. My usual FBI partner, Nick Radowski, was still nursing wounds that he'd suffered when a bomb exploded near him during the Boston Marathon. That was several weeks back. He was close to returning, even said he looked forward to kicking my ass in a race. Our competitiveness helped drive each other.

Ozzie Novak came to mind. A dear friend, a kindred spirit. He was a private investigator, was built like someone who wore a mask and a cape, and cared for my family deeply. Hell, he'd saved Luke and Erin and his own daughter, Mackenzie, when my old home had been destroyed in a bombing. But he was back in

Austin, Texas, right now, trying to piece together his life with his daughter. His wife had been killed almost two months earlier. So, he wasn't an option, either. I couldn't reach out to anyone else in the law-enforcement community, including Jerry, my boss and also a good friend. The risk was too high.

I knew I'd be singing a different tune if this were happening to someone else. But when it's your own child, your mind operates in a mode that can't be easily explained, as if it's on auto-pilot—to find my baby girl, to rescue her, to keep her safe.

I just wondered how the hell that was supposed to happen. What was this task that the caller had mentioned to the Faulks? I knew there had to be at least two people involved, since the Faulks were on their call at the same time I was on mine. Why were the stories different? Maybe the two kidnappers hadn't rehearsed what they were going to say. Maybe my kidnapper was so enthralled by the prospect of getting two million bucks, he went straight to the money. Whereas, the Faulks' contact was more methodical and knew the next step in the process was to have me complete some task.

A task. Maybe there was no discrepancy between the calls—maybe my "task" was simply to get here and bring the two million bucks. However, I wasn't exactly trusting my logical side right now. It seemed like I was attached to a massive pendulum. At times, my brain surged with oxygen to the point I thought my head might explode. Then, sometimes just seconds later, it felt like my air passages had been cut off and I might suffocate.

"Fuck!" I yelled as a jet screamed overhead.

I was bumped from behind.

A man in flip-flops and a T-shirt that read *"I'm going to get fucked in Vegas"* was too busy high-fiving two other guys as they walked out of the airport to notice me. I smelled booze as they passed. A movie zipped to the front of my mind for a quick second: *The Hangover*, part five or six or whatever sequel they were on. The men laughed as they crossed the street heading for the parking lot. I was certain their trip would be nothing but a blur.

Where was I supposed to go? Had my kidnapper given me more specific advice and I'd forgotten it?

At just forty-one years old, was I already having memory issues? That's what it felt like. I could only recall him saying that I'd get further instructions once I got here. But from whom? I eyed clusters of people, young and old, and wondered if they were tied to this kidnapping group.

Out of nowhere, a memory of Erin shot across the mental bow, back when she was two years old, her head covered with tight, blond curls. It was summertime, and she was frolicking in the little plastic pool that I'd just filled with water. She was talking to herself in a language only she could understand. And she was having a blast.

Damn, I missed those times. So innocent and yet so free. She was always within a safe environment. Fast forward fourteen years, I'd allowed her to go with Becca and her parents to Las Vegas for spring break. Vegas. Sin City. I knew perverts and bad people were everywhere—hell, I'd collared more than my fair share up and down the East Coast, even some in Texas—but what was I thinking? I'd just let her start dating a month ago.

My phone buzzed. I jerked it to eye level. A text.

Take a cab to South Mojave and Olive and get out. More instructions once u r there. Ten minutes.

I looked up and saw a yellow cab at the curb. I reached the sedan at the same time as two girls wearing tube tops far too small for their endowments. "Our cab, old lady. You can take the next one," the girl in the bouncing orange top said, one hand on the door handle. "Maybe one of those geriatric buses will come along, and you can be lifted into the bus in a wheelchair." They giggled.

I didn't. "Get your fucking hand off the door handle before I break it."

The girl—actually, her breasts—moved to within an inch of my face. Was this about to go down, right now?

"I don't see Wonder Woman around here, biyatch," she said, wagging a finger in my face. "So you better back off, or me and my friend are going to teach you a lesson in—"

I grabbed her finger and twisted it and her wrist before she could utter another word. Her shriek caused a few heads to turn, but it was Vegas, so people had to be used to extreme everything. "Get the hell away from the cab, or I'll keep twisting until I break about twenty bones."

"Okay, okay, okay," she squealed, standing on her toes.

I let go, jumped into the back seat, and leaned forward to the cabbie.

"Shit, lady, you're either badass or you got a screw loose. Either way, Vegas is the town for you, I can tell you that right now."

I smacked the seat in front me. "Get me to the corner of South Mojave and Olive. Five minutes."

"It will take me at least ten," he said, looking into the mirror.

"Fifty bucks extra if you can make it in five."

He punched the gas.

Four

The cabbie jerked the car to a stop, threw the gearshift into park, and gave me a toothy grin in the rearview—as in, a single front tooth.

"Four minutes, forty-eight seconds." He sounded gassed, as if he'd just run the five-mile trip.

I handed him seventy dollars. "Appreciate you breaking the law for me."

"Eh. Around here, breaking the law is more of an honor than a risk."

I shut the door, and he sped away. The corner of South Mojave and Olive—located in east Vegas, far off the bustling strip—for some reason took my mind to the TV show *Breaking Bad*. Maybe it was the sad excuses for homes, where at least one car was up on cinderblocks in every other lot. Or maybe it was the rundown apartment buildings with rust seemingly part of the design scheme.

Another feeling washed over me. One of loneliness. I was surrounded by a lot of structures, but as I looked around, I saw no sign of any people. Well, I did see some laundry flapping from a wire in someone's front lawn—yes, the front lawn. Other than that, the area was abandoned. Maybe everyone worked at night, when all the tourists were spending money at the height of their inebriation. Maybe this desolate feeling was just business as usual in east Vegas.

I checked my phone. Still had about a minute until the deadline. But I wondered where this odyssey would take me next. I typed in a text to Brad.

At the corner of S Mojave and Olive in Vegas. Awaiting more instructions.

Standing at the corner, I did a slow three-sixty, finishing the loop as a car pulled up to the stop sign. It was a pimped-out version of a Honda Accord. Gold paint glittered, the windows were more like mirrors, and the thud of the bass from inside the car made the shell of the car quake. It was that loud.

Was this the kidnapper—nothing more than a street thug?

I bent over, put my hands on my knees, and looked toward the window. A second later, the car sped off. Perhaps they'd been scared away by my "old woman" looks.

My phone vibrated. A quick glance to see a reply from Brad.

Thx for the intel. Just know I'm right there by you every step of the way. You will get Erin home.

Damn, he was always so positive. But he also knew I needed to read it.

Another buzz on my phone. The same number that had sent me the text at the airport.

Walk north on Mojave. Turn into mobile home park. Go to last one on the left.

Somehow the kidnapper knew I'd made it on time. Maybe my one-tooth cabbie was part of this scheme. Or the driver of the funky Honda. Or someone could be watching me from one of the nearby homes or apartments. Who knew? I did as the text said and moved at the pace of a speed-walker. Still took me three minutes, but I made it to the edge of La Villa Vegas Mobile Home Park. I avoided a pothole that could have swallowed a VW

Bug and entered the fenced-in lot. As expected, mobile homes of various sizes were situated every few feet. Some were larger, a few had Astroturf just outside their doors, and a couple had fancy awnings, which were probably worth more than the mobile homes.

I had one central question at this point: was Erin in the last mobile home on the left?

I followed the narrow road as it curved around a small bend and then was able to see the back of the park. A small mobile home—one that had smeared rust on the sides—sat all alone, not another mobile home within fifty feet. Maybe they'd picked this one on purpose, in case the girls started screaming. I moved closer and instinctively nudged my arm against my torso, hoping to feel the weight of my gun. Of course, it wasn't there. I should have stopped at a pawn shop and purchased one. But with what time? The kidnappers might have had that in mind when they gave me this tight timeline.

Moving within about a hundred feet, I got the sense there were eyes on me. Were they kidnapper eyes, though? I wasn't sure. He sent me to this mobile home for a reason. Did it relate to the "task" the Faulks' caller had mentioned? It had to be connected to getting the kidnappers the ransom money, right? I was trying to piece together something that made sense, to think like a kidnapper.

My pulse did a drumroll on the side of my neck, but my legs didn't stop moving. Part of me wondered if I was walking right into a trap. But then my thoughts switched to what Erin might be feeling right now. Was she trying to be strong? Did she have hope for rescue? Or had she given up?

No, Erin. Don't give up. I'm coming, baby girl.

My mind went through a few tactical questions as I got close enough to see all the windows covered from the inside with what appeared to be aluminum foil. Were the girls tied up? Were they on the floor? Were their eyes covered? How many kidnappers were inside? Did they have weapons?

Did you go through training in Quantico? Of course they have weapons, Alex.

I swallowed, but my mouth was pasty. I wanted water. But I wanted my daughter back more.

I reached the mobile home, paused a second to see if someone might open the door. *Do I knock or just walk in?* I glanced at my phone. No messages. I rapped my knuckles three times on the hollow door and stepped back a couple of feet, since the door opened outward.

No response. I didn't pick up a single sound. Was this another false alarm?

I took in a breath, put my hand on the doorknob, and slowly turned my wrist. The door wasn't locked.

Just then, a dog barked, breaking the silence like a reaper's scythe. I turned my head but didn't see a dog. Maybe it was at a neighboring mobile home. Or was it on the other side of the fence? As long as it wasn't chewing on my leg, I was good.

I slowly pulled the door open. It was dark inside. The sunlight illuminated some type of built-in table and booth.

"Erin?" I called out.

No response. My joints felt like they were coated with rust. *Dammit, I wish I had my Glock on me.*

I slowly walked up two wooden stairs and took one step into the home.

The door slammed shut behind me, engulfing me in darkness. I jumped but landed in an athletic position—knees bent, both arms up, ready to take on anything that came my way. But I couldn't see a damn thing.

I went still, even held my breath for a second. Nothing.

I exhaled.

And then there was something. Footsteps against the hollow floors—many, as in more than one person.

"Erin?" I didn't think it was her. The steps sounded too heavy. "Please let me see—"

A fist the size of a turkey clocked my jaw, and I fell back. My spine hit the edge of the table, and I crumbled to the side. I literally saw stars.

Down on all fours, I blinked and wiped my face, hoping to regain my mental faculties. I didn't get the chance. A second later, I felt a sharp zap at the base of my spine. My limbs felt on fire, and I lost all control of my muscles. Falling to the floor like a fish thrown onto a dock, my body began to convulse. I'd been hit with a Taser.

I wanted to speak, to ask what they were doing, how this would help them get their ransom money, and where Erin and Becca were. But nothing came out. I was alive, but I didn't feel like a lifeform.

The convulsions subsided, and I took in a breath. I realized I was sweating like a pig. I could sense more than one person near me, but my eyes couldn't make out how many or their sizes.

"C-can I see my daughter?" I sputtered.

"You'll see plenty in a few minutes."

It was a man.

A burlap sack was dropped over my head. I didn't fight it. A needle punctured my neck. Within seconds, I grew very tired. Someone picked me up, tossed me over their shoulder like a bag of peat moss. I tried to move, to grab the guy by the neck, but I was slowly losing consciousness. The door to the trailer opened. Through the sack, light blared into my eyes, but even that couldn't wake me from this trance. A moment later, I was dumped into the trunk of a car.

BACK AT YOU

I smelled gasoline, and then I fell asleep.

Five

I woke up in a hallway, propped up in a corner. A few breaths to remind me I was still alive. I picked up a sickening waft...something sour and musty. My stomach was doing flip-flops. I tried to wipe my face, but it was more of a smack. My tongue was dry and felt like it had doubled in size. I needed water.

Where was Erin? I heard distant voices. Some were agitated. Men, women...maybe some who didn't speak English. My mind felt like it had been dunked in oily sludge.

Was someone grunting? I squinted, tried to get a better view of my surroundings. A long hall to my left, a shorter one to my right that ended with an industrial-looking metal door. Back to the left. I saw doorways on both sides of the corridor.

Something flapped from a doorway. A curtain?

I moved away from the wall, and my body rocked precariously, like a pencil that was trying to gain balance standing on one end. I rested my palms on the floor. A worn, gray rug, covered in dust and dirt. Gross.

With my arms in place to anchor my body, I peered up and saw black curtains hanging at each doorway. No doors, just curtains.

More grunting mixed with male and female voices. I wanted

to call out for Erin, but something told me to hold off. I got to my knees, opened my jaw—and the excruciating pain hit me. I recalled the blow to my face back in the trailer. And then the Taser, the convulsions, the shot in the neck, and being thrown in the trunk of a car.

Whatever. I was still breathing. I could still save Erin and Becca. I started crawling down the hall. I got to the first curtained doorway and peered inside. A woman was gyrating on top of a man. He was cussing at her, but she didn't seem to care. She had on a slinky, see-through robe that was opened. She was casually smoking a cigarette, as if she were at a bar doing a little people watching. She had to be a prostitute. I kept crawling, made it to the next room. I saw a hairy guy with a gut so large it hid his genitals—thank God. He was getting dressed. A young girl was still lying in the bed, a sheet pulled up to her chest. She stared at the ceiling, her eyes glazed over. I could hear the man breathing as if he had just one lung, each movement a strain.

My gut twisted into a knot. Is this what they had Erin and Becca doing? I knew the girls wouldn't…couldn't do this on their own. Erin had dated for the first time only recently. What was this kidnapping really all about?

Seething anger pushed tears into my eyes.

In the hallway, using the wall as leverage, I somehow maneuvered my way up to my feet. Slightly more lucid, I heard more groans and conversations—some in English, some in Spanish, maybe another language or two in there. I wasn't certain. I had to get help. Cops, FBI could raid this place, find Erin and Becca, and put an end to everything.

While leaning against the wall, I shuffled my way down the corridor and stopped just shy of another doorway. A large hand pushed back the curtain, and a man stepped into the hallway. He eye-checked me for a second. Bags hung under his eyes like cocoon nests. He looked back over his shoulder into the room. "Same time next week, Daisy?"

"Sure. Whatever you want, Herman. I'm always here for you."

The girl had an accent—French, Italian, I couldn't tell—and the excitement of a mortician.

Herman took another look at me but said nothing. He walked off, hooked a left, and then I heard a door open. That metal door had to be the exit. I peeked into the room, and the girl snagged my gaze. "Are you my next customer?" she asked casually, as if she were going to give me a manicure.

I *think* I shook my head. I felt frozen in place, mortified.

"Come on now, don't be shy." She patted the mattress next to her. "I don't judge. I like women…especially mature women, not these young girls they have running around here."

It seemed as though a hundred-pound weight had been dropped on my chest. This girl didn't appear legal to vote, and she was talking about younger girls? All I could think about was the last time I looked into Erin's eyes just before she drove off with the Faulks. Her blue eyes mirrored mine almost exactly. Her skin was porcelain, flawless and pure. She'd grown up over the last few months, losing a little bit of the attitude, but she was still so naïve about the world. And that was the way it should be at the age of sixteen.

My eyes had been darting around, but I focused on the girl. She might have seen Erin and Becca, or at least heard someone mention their names.

"Can you—"

"Wait." The girl sat up in the bed and pulled a sheet over her chest. "Are you a cop or something?"

I pushed some hair out of my face, looked down, and saw my shirt untucked and wrinkled. What about my appearance made her believe I was a cop? "Not sure where you got that fwum."

What the hell? Fwum?

She looked at me with suspicious eyes. "You high or something?"

I wasn't sure how to answer the question. My jaw hung open as my brain fought to find the right words. "No," I finally said. "Hey, I'm looking for…"

She lurched out of her position with the quickness of a panther, on all fours at the end of the bed. "Bitch, I know you got some tango and cash. Give it up, come on," she said, extending an arm. Her pupils were dime-sized. I could barely see any whites in her eyes.

"I don't have anything," I said, pulling back before losing my balance. I fell against the wall on the other side of the hall, but managed to stay upright.

"Daisy will do anything for that tango and cash. Come on now. I know you got some. I can see it in your eyes."

Tango and cash… Wasn't that a movie? I shook my head and lumbered away, hoping she wouldn't chase after me. I made it another ten feet and could hear her barking at me, most of it in four-letter words. I wondered if all the girls in these rooms were strung out like Daisy.

I stopped in my tracks. Why didn't I think of this earlier? Erin might be in any of these rooms. Maybe Becca too. I could see the metal door just around the corner, but I backtracked and began looking inside each room. Girls were servicing their customers in the first two rooms on the right. Then I passed Daisy's room. She was on the floor, her head between her knees, muttering something under her breath. Was she going through some type of withdrawal?

My equilibrium improved, and I shuffled past her doorway unnoticed. I heard a squeal—it went straight to my heart. That was the same noise Erin made whenever she and Luke would get into a tickle-fight. It was coming from the door on the left. I edged closer. Part of me wanted to pull back the curtain and find her. But there was also a part of me that couldn't take it if I found Erin in the same demeaning position as Daisy and the other girls. Fear wrapped its cold fingers around my throat.

If this is Erin, it's not really the same girl. She's a victim, drugged, coerced. No choice.

My breath quaked as I pulled back the curtain. It was a girl—and she was with two guys. I almost threw up. The two guys looked at me and didn't do anything more than shrug. If I had a fucking gun, I would have put bullets right between their eyes. I threw the curtain back and moved on to the other rooms. No Erin. No Becca. But lots of other girls with guys.

Rage fueled me now. Running my hand down the side of the wall to ensure I didn't tumble over, I marched down the corridor, took a left, and pushed open the metal door.

A man the size of Sasquatch was standing over me. I looked up. All I saw was the face of Richard Nixon.

Six

I sat at a kitchen table that wobbled every time I shifted my hands. The two men—one on either side of me—had told me to keep my hands on the table. My wrists were bound together with plastic ties, which cut into my skin, though the pain barely registered. Every few seconds, I brought the water bottle they'd given me up to my mouth and took a few chugs.

The mammoth man who wore a cartoonish mask of Nixon had been with me the whole time. He spoke very few words. He was the one who'd tied my wrists and then picked me up like I was a toddler and sat me in the chair. I'd been in the kitchen for about ten minutes. Just a second ago, Jimmy Carter had joined us. The pretend Carter wasn't a big guy, just average. But he was the talker—or more to the point, the instructor.

"You will follow the instructions I've given you exactly. Do you understand me, Alex Troutt?" His accent was Eastern European, and he enunciated each word precisely.

"Yes." My voice was measured, even though my mind still felt like it was tangled in a web of sticky goo. I caught a glimpse of Carter's hands. They appeared soft, as if he'd recently had a manicure. He was wearing designer jeans, and he sat with one leg crossed over the other, casual, as if it were just another night at the symphony. Even though the whole place smelled like a litter box, I picked up a waft of fine cologne. I could tell my brain was short-circuiting on the strange combination of Carter's refined characteristics in this trashy environment. The structure was a one-story home that had been remodeled to fit their particular business interests—a prostitution ring and drug prison, from what I'd seen.

Carter smacked his hands on his thighs and stood up. "So, let's wait another hour for you to have your mind working properly, and we will review the instructions one more time. Then you will be on your way."

I was happy to have the extra hour, allowing my brain and body to heal. All the while, my eyes scoured the kitchen looking for a possible weapon. I only saw bags of fast food on the counters and floor. No signs of a knife, although I wondered if one of the drawers contained flatware. Surely, they had to have forks, spoons, and table knives.

Then again, what about this experience was normal?

An hour clocked by, and I continued my surveillance, listened for Erin's voice, and waited. Nixon and Carter didn't say a word, though I did notice Carter checking the time on his watch, which appeared to be rimmed in diamonds. "To reiterate what I told you earlier," Carter said after the hour had passed, "you will go to the address listed on this slip of paper." He tapped the table next to the piece of paper. The table wobbled. "The directions on how to get there are on the other side. When you get there, go to the back door, tell them your first and last name. They will give you two boxes. Put them in the trunk and then drive back here."

"You haven't told me where *there* is or where *here* is. I guess I'm still in Vegas, right?"

Carter lifted his head, as if he were looking over my shoulder toward Nixon. I couldn't tell exactly. All I could see were small holes in the mask for eyes, which looked like black marbles. The mask fluttered about as he moved and spoke. It was creepy, watching the cartoonish jowls flop around like water balloons. While part of me wanted to rip the masks off both of them, I considered the fact that they were hiding their identities to be a positive sign. They didn't want me to identify them. I had no idea who they were. That gave me some hope. I could pick up the boxes and then trade them for the girls and go. Skepticism, though, hadn't left me.

"You will find out soon enough when we take you out to the car. But, yes, you are in Las Vegas, although not in the actual city limits. We are on a ten-acre piece of property. Not many trees, but a fence and a large, grassy knoll provide us the necessary privacy we need to conduct our business."

A business. As if this was registered with the Better Business Bureau. Oh, how I wanted to ask him some pointed questions. But I knew this wasn't an FBI interrogation room. I didn't have the upper hand. I was lucky to be breathing. I had to play this smart…well, as smart as I could. Anything to get Erin and Becca out of here alive.

I leaned forward, eyed the address on the paper. "This is only a street address. Where am I going?"

Carter reached into his pocket, pulled out a small cell phone, and gently set it next to the piece of paper. "You will use this to be in contact with us."

He hadn't answered my question. But I suddenly realized I didn't have my phone on me. A moment later, Nixon got up, walked over to a trash can, and dangled my phone just above it. He let it swing between his thumb and forefinger before dropping it to the floor. "Oops," he said, bringing a hand to the front of his fake mouth. He then used the heel of his boot to crack my phone into pieces. He scooped up the remnants and dropped them in the trash.

"So," Carter said as Nixon sat back down, "this phone will be how you stay in contact with us. We expect updates on your status every hour, top of the hour. And no other calls or text messages to anyone."

They were doing everything in their power to cut me off from my world of contacts. I felt isolated, vulnerable. They knew they had control over me and my actions, but I couldn't play it completely weak.

"You never answered my question. Where am I going?"

"Los Angeles. Near LAX airport." Carter flipped the paper over and tapped it. "Directions are on this side. You only need to use the phone to give us status updates."

I could hear my breath flutter. LA? That had to be five or six hours away. No way in hell I was driving ten hours without my Erin. But how could I win over Carter and Nixon?

"I'm assuming these two boxes are worth a lot of money to you."

No verbal response, just some head movements and flapping masks. Surely, when this was all over, I would have nightmares, like with the clowns in the classic Stephen King novel, *It*.

"One of you—I'm assuming it was one of you called and talked about receiving two million dollars in ransom…" I paused and made sure my battered mind didn't mention the call from the Faulks. I didn't want Carter and Nixon to learn that I'd been in contact with anyone. "Whatever is in these two boxes, that will fulfill the ransom request?"

"You better hope so." It was Nixon who'd answered. He had no distinct accent to his voice. But he didn't sound as educated as his counterpart.

"Richard!" Carter said in a rebuking tone.

Damn, this whole presidential theme was strange.

"Sorry, Jimmy. I just want the—"

"Don't say another word," Carter said.

Nixon held up two hands. "Whatever. You're the boss."

That confirmed what I'd thought. Now that I knew the organizational hierarchy—at least with the people in my purview—I continued my quest to try to end this before someone got hurt. Then again, how did I know Erin and Becca were still alive? Somehow, I kept my tears at bay, although the mere thought chipped off a piece of my heart.

"So, as you can see, I've followed your instructions ever since you called me."

"More or less," Carter said.

I wasn't going to start building my case, but I sensed he could see that I was treating this as a negotiation. He was sharp. Maybe too sharp.

"As an act of good faith, I'd like to take Erin and Becca with me on this errand. I will not talk to anyone, as you instructed. I will follow through and bring the boxes to you."

Carter snorted out a laugh. He paused, looked at his nails. He couldn't contain himself. He broke out in a cackle that made the hair on my arms stand up. Nixon joined in, and the laughter went on for a good minute. Finally, Carter rose to his feet, walked a few steps, and then flipped around, pointing a finger at me.

"You think with your Jedi FBI tricks that you can fool us, Alex Troutt?" He shook his head. "Your ego is something to behold. Even with the lives of your daughter and her friend on the line, you still want to act like you're in control." He picked up a chair and slammed it to the floor.

Nixon and I both flinched.

"You fucking Americans are all alike."

"I'm not like that, Jimmy. Come on now. Don't group us all together."

"Shut the fuck up!"

Silence filled the small room. A moment later, I picked up faint sounds of more grunting and groaning through a wall. Disgusting.

Carter flipped a hand toward his underling. "Play her the recording."

"Will do. This should be fun," Nixon said, pulling a phone out of his pocket.

An icy patch formed on the back of my neck as my breaths came out in short gasps.

Nixon fumbled with his phone.

"Play it, now!" Carter's composure had been cracked like an egg. He seemed unhinged.

"Okay, okay," Nixon said. He placed the phone on the table and tapped a button.

I heard muffled voices. Then...

"Leave me the fuck alone, you fucking prick!"

It was Erin. Every muscle and joint in my body turned to stone.

Then a scream. That had to be Becca.

"Leave her the fuck alone," Erin said.

And then another scream—that was Erin.

Loud voices erupted, male and female, followed by yelling and shuffling.

I started to lift out of my seat. "Did you fucking harm my child?"

Carter motioned with his hand for me to sit. I didn't, but Nixon grabbed my arm and yanked me down.

It was all I could do not to lash out and start pounding on Nixon. But I knew it would be counterproductive. My hands were still bound, and Nixon would swat me away like a fly. I had to sit there and listen.

A second later, Erin released a shrill that made my insides explode. I grabbed the empty water bottle and crushed it. Then, from the phone: "Get away. No. Don't. Don't put that in me. I'll do anything. I'll listen, I'll do whatever. Just don't put that needle in my arm. No, no, noooo!" She wailed a few seconds, and then it faded as though a howling wind had taken a life away.

Nixon tapped his phone and removed it from the table.

Tears filled my eyes. My whole body quaked. I couldn't make myself stop.

"Now, Alex Troutt," Carter said, his arms leaning on the back of a chair that faced me, "I'm assuming you have the motivation to carry out this task with no further questions on your part."

I lifted my eyes, my heart in pieces. "I'll do whatever you need me to do."

"Ten hours," he said, walking toward a door. "Nixon. Take her to the car. It's time to get this trip underway."

Seven

Ivy Nash

My phone buzzed, and I picked it up to see a text from Cristina, my younger partner in my small PI firm, ECHO.

What kind of beef jerky do u like?

I shook my head. I was sitting in my car outside of a RaceTrac gas station a couple of miles from our office, which was just south of downtown San Antonio. She was inside the convenience store and, as usual, she felt like she had to use her toy—her cell phone—to communicate via text. She couldn't simply walk outside and ask me, or even just give me a ring. Had to be the text.

She was ten years my junior—she'd graduated high school just a few months ago—but at times, it seemed like we'd been born a century apart.

I wasn't a big fan of texting. Well, a few words here or there were fine. Like with Saul, my boyfriend of more than a year. And those text messages had turned into the type of utterings usually reserved for late-night whispers while sharing the same pillow.

Another vibration from my phone.

Beef jerky alert. Hello????

"Will you stop it already with the texting?" I said, holding up the phone, knowing Cristina couldn't hear me. What was the deal with the beef jerky, anyway? She knew I didn't like that crap. I wasn't even sure *she* did, now that I thought about it. But she'd just turned nineteen years old. She'd been known to flip-flop on decisions. It came with the age.

I typed in a quick response. *No thanks. U almost ready?*

I waited a moment for the three dots to flash across the screen, but nothing happened. Had she been distracted from texting? Hmm. Maybe her phone battery had died.

I pointed the air-conditioning vent in my direction. It was spring—nothing like the sweltering heat we would experience in July and August—but it was still in the mid-eighties, not a cloud in the sky. As the air cooled my neck and face, I tried to look through the store windows and spot Cristina. She was just under my height of five-six, with sand-colored skin and dark hair, which, when not put up in a ponytail, hung to her mid-back. She had that tomboy look, although in the last few months, I could see she was maturing into a young woman, at least in some respects.

Me, on the other hand…I could practically glow in the dark. That was the running joke that Saul had directed at me. We'd just returned from a vacation, my first in…forever. My friends had been encouraging me to take a break from my work and go relax on a beach. Actually, *"encouraging me"* would be an understatement. It was more like begging me. They claimed they could literally feel the tension radiating off me like a portable heater. Guilt was my constant companion, though, and taking time away from our investigations—which centered on helping kids who were in danger, from the unforgiving world or sometimes themselves—had always won the battle in my mind.

Well, until Saul had picked me up for a late dinner on a Friday night. Except he didn't stop at the restaurant. He drove us all the way to Galveston, where we boarded an enormous ship. We ended up taking a seven-day Caribbean cruise. We spent the time taking in new cultures, hiking, lying on beaches, and to be perfectly honest, rocking the ship.

Yes, Ivy Nash, the woman who not only didn't have time for vacations and had previously sworn off having a serious boyfriend, made it official on that vacation. She'd used the "L" word…verbally, not just in her head.

In fact, according to Saul, after I'd imbibed in a couple of mai tais in Puerto Rico, I whispered in his ear that I wanted him to sire my children. My response to this revelation? "I'd never use the word 'sire.'" We laughed, kissed, and did our best to tip the ship on its side. After spending a majority of my life running from monsters, both as a foster child and as an adult, I'd hit a new level of euphoria I never thought possible for myself. I was in love and could see a future with Saul.

"Is that Cristina over by the beer cooler?" I said aloud as I peered through the windshield.

I squinted my eyes. Yep. That was her. What made her think she could get away with buying beer? Had she acquired a fake ID? She knew I wouldn't approve of that. Technically, I was just her employer, but the line for feeling responsible for her well-being was very thin for me. It was similar to that of a close relative. I was okay with "older sister," although she'd called me a "nagging mom" more than once. Still, though, did she think she was going to pick up a six-pack and drink it on the way to our meeting?

I checked the time. We had ten minutes to reach the office of the assistant superintendent of the San Antonio School District. They wanted an outside firm to conduct new background checks on all teachers—"can't be too careful in this day and age," I was told over the phone. The gig wasn't exactly in our wheelhouse, but it paid the bills in between the meatier cases.

I put a hand on the car door handle, just waiting for Cristina to pull open the glass door to the beer cooler.

A second later, she did exactly that. "What the hell does she think she's doing?" I hopped out of the car just as a man rushed out of the RaceTrac. His sweat-coated hair was matted to his forehead, his unblinking eyes darting around like he was high on something. Both hands gripped countless plastic bags, almost as though he'd done his complete grocery shopping...at a convenience store.

His eyes caught mine. I quickly looked past him to find Cristina. She was reviewing her choice of beer. I shut the car door and walked toward the curb. The man zipped past me and opened the rear door of a small SUV.

That was when I heard the screams of a little girl.

No big deal, right? Kids cried all the time.

But I still looked over my shoulder as I approached the door to the building. The girl was in the back seat—maybe seven or eight years old—and she appeared to be trying to get out of the vehicle, which I noticed was running. Maybe he'd left the AC on for her while he was inside.

I heard him say "no" more than few times, but I didn't hear the girl's name. Did he know her name? I assumed she was his daughter. I knew kids could be stinkers—even at the age of nineteen, apparently. I shifted my gaze back to the store, keen on finding Cristina.

I couldn't help it, though. Just as I entered the store, I flipped around to look again at the man and girl. Daughter or no daughter, if that guy took a swing at her, I'd have to confront him. After the beatings I received as a kid, I'd made a personal pledge never to let that happen to any child, if I could help it. And in this public setting, I could—*would*—stop it. Right now, though, he seemed to be consoling the girl, who was crying.

Okay, good.

I stopped at the end of a small aisle. "Cristina Tafoya!" I said, crossing my arms over my chest.

She turned around with a smile on her face, but she lost it in the blink of an eye. She didn't say a word.

"You really thought you could get away with buying beer?"

She narrowed her eyes. Wait—was she nudging her head?

"Cristina, we're going to be late for our meeting. If we get this gig, we can pay the office rent for the next five months."

She gave me more odd head movements, and her eyes were bugging out at me. Whatever.

I took another glance over my shoulder to check on the little one. The man shoved the girl into the back seat and slammed the door shut. Something was off. I just wasn't sure if it crossed the line into my business.

Back to Cristina. She was still standing there with the door to the beer cooler open. A young man was trying to get in to pick up some beer. I pointed over her shoulder. "You might want to move to let the gentleman get inside the cooler."

Cristina rolled her eyes.

Now what did I do? She might as well be speaking in tongues.

The man turned to me and extended his hand. "I'm Brice. You must be Ivy." His white teeth looked like slotted glow sticks.

"How do you know my name?" I asked with a tentative handshake.

"Cristina and I have been talking for a few minutes. Feels like we've been friends for months." He chuckled and gave her a quick wink. She laughed too, almost reflexively. Was this the same Cristina? My Cristina was usually *in your face*. Some might say she was a little rough around the edges. I'd seen her softer side, especially around the kids we helped, but this flirtatious, silly thing with the hunk of the month....hell, maybe she'd already downed a beer.

I did a quick once-over of Brice. Tank top, khaki shorts, muscles on top of more muscles, and a model-like smile.

"By the way," Brice said, "you don't have to worry about Cristina buying alcohol. Cristina told me she's nineteen. I just turned twenty-one. I'm a junior at UTSA."

"He plays tight end for the Road Runners." The tone of Cristina's voice was like a smitten schoolgirl. I was beginning to feel like this was some type of out-of-body experience. Cristina was far too streetwise to fall for some pretty boy. On top of that, she'd recently been dating another person—a girl. One who had more tats and piercings than Brice had muscles.

One word came to mind: *fickle*. That was Cristina.

I felt my phone buzz, and it obviously wasn't Cristina texting me. Maybe it was Saul. Now that I thought about it, didn't we have some type of city event we had to attend tonight?

As I lifted my phone, I heard a symphony of beeps all around me.

It was an Amber Alert. I read the message on my phone.

Seguin, TX AMBER Alert: LIC / JSG2908 (TX) Late model Red Nissan Rogue

Seguin was thirty-five miles east of San Antonio. I jerked my head around to look out to the parking lot. The man was backing his car away from the curb. It was a red SUV. And I picked up the last three digits of the license plate: 908.

I grabbed Cristina and ran to my car.

Eight

Ivy

By the time Cristina and I reached my car, the red Rogue was at the exit to the gas station. The man behind the wheel flipped his head around and looked at us. Then he peeled away, hooking a right onto the street.

"What are we doing?" Cristina asked from the other side of Black Beauty—my nickname for my old Honda Civic.

"Amber Alert. Get in," I said, slipping into the front seat. I started the car as Cristina shut the door.

"Oh yeah," she said, looking at her phone. "I got the same message. What does this have to do with us?"

"I'm almost certain the guy who kidnapped the little girl just tore out of the parking lot."

"Almost certain?"

Pushback. Just what I needed.

"Call nine-one-one, give them our location, tell them we're tailing the guy who was just mentioned in the Amber Alert."

"But where is he?" She swiveled her head left and right.

I ignored her for a moment as I pulled out of the lot and punched the gas. I could see the red vehicle pass through a green light just ahead.

"Red car, just in front of us."

"Right. I see him." Cristina tapped the phone a few times, put it to her ear. "Yeah," she said into the phone. "Want to report that my friend and I just spotted the car in the Amber Alert." A brief pause.

"Put it on speaker phone," I said, increasing my speed.

Cristina tapped the screen and held it between us. Just then, the light turned yellow. I pressed the gas pedal to the floor and leaned my back against the seat. The light turned red. I was already moving at over fifty miles an hour. I saw a truck to my right enter the intersection. "Hold on!"

"What the fuuuck!" Cristina yelled as I swerved left. The truck jerked to a stop as horns blared all around us.

But we made it through unscathed. "Sorry," I said, with a quick glance in my rearview.

"What is going on?" the operator asked.

"Just trying to catch up to the pervert who has that little girl in the back seat of his Rogue," I said.

"Where are you?" she asked

Traffic congested the roads. I tapped the brakes, swung across two lanes to get past a slower car, and then cut around a garbage truck and sped up. The Rogue was up ahead but seemed farther away now.

"Uh, we're on Aransas," Cristina said. "We went right out of the gas station."

"Right? Sweetie, I need more information than that."

I jumped in. "We're heading west. We just passed the Palmetto intersection."

"Thank you. Let me put this in the system."

There was a pause for a few seconds. I continued swinging Black Beauty in and out of the lanes. I got lucky at the next intersection and hit a green light—albeit at a high rate of speed.

"Look out!" Cristina yelled.

A massive RV pulled onto the road. No time to break—I jerked the steering wheel to the left.

A horn from behind me. I looked in my blind spot and saw a silver pickup twisting as it hit the brakes. Just inches before we barreled into the RV, I squeezed my Civic through the small opening.

"Damn, you're a crazy woman. Have I told you that?" Cristina shouted. I caught a glance of her face—it was almost as white as mine.

"Please don't put yourself or other motorists in danger," the operator said.

Cristina and I traded a quick glance. No way would I let this pervert get away. God knew what he'd do to her once he found a safe spot away from anyone who could protect the little girl. I'd been abused throughout my seventeen stops in my foster-home tour. This abuser we could stop—we *had* to stop.

"He just hooked a left," Cristina said.

"Where?" the operator asked.

"Uh…" Cristina looked at me. She didn't know directions, not unless she used her phone.

"It's Hackberry. We turned south."

"Thanks." The operator paused a few seconds and then said, "We have units en route."

I executed the left-hand turn and could now fully see the license plate on the back of Rogue. We were closing in—the traffic must have slowed him down.

"He's right there," Cristina said, smacking a hand against the dashboard. "Come on, get this hunk of shit moving."

Just after avoiding a hoard of cyclists, I saw I-10 up ahead. I knew if the man in the Rogue made it to the interstate, he'd be able to leave my old Civic in the dust, and then he'd likely jump off at an exit and get lost in the city until things died down. We only had a few seconds to stop him.

"He can't get on the interstate heading that way." Christina pointed to her right—which was west.

The Rogue's brakes lights turned red. "He's going under the overpass. Probably going to turn left and hop on the interstate going east."

"East, yeah," Cristina said.

I passed a small side street and noticed a police car with its lights on.

"Here comes the cavalry," Cristina said, looking over her shoulder.

"The what?" the operator said from the phone.

I jerked my car left.

"You're in the wrong lane!" Cristina yelled.

I knew it was my only chance to catch the pervert. Cars veered away from me as I held down the horn and sped forward while everyone else was braking.

"You're not going to…" Cristina anchored a hand on the car roof and started yelling.

I didn't hit the brakes until the Rogue began to turn left onto the frontage road. I veered left—aiming to cut off his path.

"What the…?" Cristina hollered.

Now just in front of the Rogue, I slammed on the brakes. He swerved right but jerked the car to a stop just as the corners of our cars tapped each other. As I swung open my door, the police car pulled to a stop on the other side of the Rogue. Two cops jumped out with guns at the ready.

"Stop, don't shoot," I said, running around Black Beauty. "There's a little girl in that car."

"Get down, lady," the cop with sunglasses yelled.

I reached the back door, but it was locked. Inside, I saw the girl crying. The cops yelled out instructions.

"Open the door," I called out to the man behind the wheel. "It's over."

He was reaching inside his glovebox.

"I think he's got a gun!" I yelled.

"Get out of the way, lady!" the cop screamed again.

I smacked my hand on the back window. "Don't do it! Don't do it!"

The man in the car pulled his hand out of the console. Did he have a gun? Fuck! Panic rippled through my body. "Stop! Don't hurt the girl," I said, pounding the window.

A second later, he got out of the car with his hands raised.

With the back door now unlocked, I swung it open. The red-faced girl was screaming uncontrollably, reaching out to me. I leaned over and unbuckled her just as I saw the cops grab the man and throw him to the ground. The girl bear-hugged me, all the while screaming. It was complete chaos.

"Are you okay?" Cristina ran up next to me.

"Fine." I held the little girl tightly as I walked around the car.

One cop had his knee in the small of the man's back. He was pulling the man's arm back and cuffing it while the other cop had his weapon aimed at the man. The cop—the one with sunglasses—glanced in my direction.

"Lady, you could have gotten yourself killed."

"Please help me," the man lying on the ground said.

"Daddy, Daddy, Daddy," the little girl yelled.

It was his daughter. Must have been a domestic issue. But he still could have been abusing her.

I tried to calm the little girl as the cop finished putting the cuffs on the man, got him to his feet, and walked him to the police car.

"I'm telling you, I was trying to save my daughter. This is a crock of shit."

"Yeah, right," the cop said. "Shut up and get inside."

"Please listen to me. My daughter is in danger. You can't take her back to her mother. Both of my daughters are…"

The cop shoved the man in the back of the police car and slammed the door shut.

The little girl cried until she had no more tears.

Nine

Alex

I stopped only once on the way to LA to use the restroom. While inside the gas station, I considered asking if I could borrow their phone. But as I saw patrons coming in and out of the store and noticed ever more people and cars bustling about outside, I wondered if Carter and Nixon might have one of their team members following me, purposely blending in to keep tabs on me.

Was I being overly paranoid? Maybe. Maybe not. My thoughts were all over the place. My usual barometer of "reading the situation" was off-kilter. Nothing about this kidnapping and ransom-related task followed a typical pattern of behavior. Then again, with Erin at the center of all this, I knew my unpredictable emotions had taken dominance over my logical brain.

I picked up a small package of donuts with the cash Carter had given me for the trip and got back into my car—a forgettable Chrysler 300 that had to be ten years old. A few minutes later, just on the north side of the City of Angels, I was snarled in traffic.

I put in my status call to Carter. With no introduction, I opened the call by saying, "I hit traffic going into LA."

"Are you following the directions?" he asked.

"Yes. But I don't know how long it's going to take me to get to this place near LAX."

"I expected as much. I'll let your contact know you'll be late."

"Are you going to tell me who this contact is?"

"You don't need to know that. The only thing you need to worry about is getting the two boxes back to the compound without incident. You do that, you get your kid back. You don't, well…" A pompous chuckle. "I think you know the answer."

"Will you at least let me talk to her on the phone?"

The line went dead.

"Fuck!" I slammed my fist against the steering wheel. Tears pooled in my eyes. For the next several minutes, while crawling along the freeway, my thoughts about Erin's safety ate a hole in my stomach.

Echoes of her screams that I'd heard on the audio recording replayed in my mind over and over again, each one ripping into my soul. I'd let her down. If there was one basic function parents were obligated to perform, it was to protect their children. Nothing else came before it. I'd spent too much of my adult life trying to pursue bad people while ignoring my own children. How could I do this to my precious Erin?

Guilt consumed me, as those screams kept clawing at my insides. I cried out loud and violently smacked the passenger seat, not stopping until I broke into a sweat and could hear my heaving breaths.

As I squeezed the steering wheel, images flashed to the front of my mind—of what Erin might be experiencing. Drugs being forced into her body. Beatings. Rape. It would not only rob her of her innocence, but the experience might completely break her…even kill her. My mind was racing out of control. If I couldn't stop the abuse, then I had to feel what Erin was feeling. The flood of pictures didn't cease. Every time a new one hit, it felt like a spear had punctured my body. The more I thought about her and what she might be going through, the more I felt myself spiraling into a dark place.

In between my sobs, I gasped for air.

Red lights snagged my attention. I pounded my foot on the brake, and the Chrysler rocked to a stop just inches from the back of a FedEx truck.

Crap. I loosened my death grip on the steering wheel and looked around me. I was surrounded by traffic. Above me, dusk had painted the sky in a deep purple. *Erin loves purple.*

I took in a deep breath and exhaled slowly. My shoulders slackened, and I could feel my unrelenting tension drop out of the red zone.

As the pace of the congested traffic picked up, I turned my thoughts about the situation to more positive ones. Erin had recently demonstrated an inner resolve and a level of maturity that, to be honest, caught me off-guard. It wasn't there all the time, but it was more than a quick flash. Some of it, I realized, was a desire to be more independent.

It was as though she'd consciously told herself, *"Show Mom you can be responsible, even deal with a little adversity, and she'll release the reins a bit."*

She'd read me perfectly—I'd done exactly as she wanted. Had I screwed up? Or was it simply the natural evolution of a girl growing into a young woman and a mom allowing her to do so? I'd been her age. At the time, my dad was a lush and I thought my mom was dead—turned out she was being held captive against her will in a cult compound. My dad pushed me, though, to be better than anyone else in tennis and in school. I kicked the asses of everyone I faced.

I recalled going to Erin's tennis match a couple of weeks back. She'd developed a killer serve, but I also saw something that shocked me. She didn't play it safe with dink-and-dunk shots like she had her first couple of years. Instead, she demonstrated this go-for-it-mentality, hitting each groundstroke with ferocious intensity. She'd win a serve game and then toss the balls to her opponent on the other side of the net with this unshakeable confidence. It had reminded me of…me.

Maybe Erin was a lot stronger than I realized. Maybe she could hold on until I got to her.

She can. She can.

Traffic broke up, and I picked up some speed. For whatever reason, my emotional outburst had emboldened me, at least for the time being. I turned on the radio to distract my thoughts. It was tuned to an AM news station. Lots of traffic reports. I was on Interstate 110 heading south. But the traffic reporter kept using the term "the" in front of every major thoroughfare. *The* 110. *The* 405. *The* 213. It was really strange. I looked up and saw a sign for Los Angeles International Airport—LAX. It was eleven miles to my west, and just beyond that was the coast. I'd always wanted to visit California. But not like this.

I hit South LA and saw signs for Huntington Park and Inglewood. I drove farther and saw more signs for South Gate, Lynwood, and Compton. Then I saw the one I was looking for—Gardena.

I exited at Marine Avenue and headed east. To my left, I saw a sign for Hustler Casino. Nice. And I thought I'd left the land of casinos back in Las Vegas.

I maneuvered through the neighborhood and pulled into a rocky driveway of a small home. It was almost completely dark now, but a single light bathed the front porch in yellow. The house wasn't falling apart, but it would never be used on any websites to draw tourists to sunny LA.

I got out of the Chrysler and looked around the neighborhood. Two men were walking a big dog at the end of the block, just two houses down. They didn't look my way. As I walked up to the porch, I could hear dogs barking in the distance. Again, I wished like hell I had my Glock on me. I knew, regardless of any impediment, I had to complete this task. If anything happened to me, then Erin and Becca would be doomed.

Don't go there, Alex.

I walked to the front door and didn't see a doorbell, so I knocked twice.

A moment later, the door opened a crack. It was dark inside, but I saw a chain above a man's head. Mostly, I saw an eyeball.

"What the fuck you doing, bitch? You're supposed to go around back."

He slammed the door shut.

Ten

Alex

Crap. I'd forgotten about the back-door part. I scooted off the porch, started up the Chrysler, and eased down the driveway. I got out of the car, passed through a fenced gate, and made my way to the back door. Before I knocked, the door opened.

"You a cop?" The man was about my height of five-six. The whites of his eyes practically glowed in the night. His brown shirt was unbuttoned to reveal a hairless, concave chest.

"What? I was sent here to pick up two boxes."

"That ain't what I asked, is it?"

I shook my head. This guy seemed highly agitated. I just wanted to pick up the boxes and get out of Gardena. Carter hadn't said anything about the person on this end possibly being trouble. Had he set me up, or at least put me in the crosshairs of a person who was not of sound mind? Maybe that was why he'd chosen me over the Faulks, because of my FBI experience. It made sense. Kind of.

"I'm not a cop. My daughter and her friend are being held captive until I bring back two boxes. I have no idea what's in the boxes—and I don't care. I just want to get the boxes to the men who sent me and get the girls back safely."

He nodded and rubbed his chin as he looked over my head. He was thinking something over, but I couldn't guess what. I spotted a patch on his shirt: US Customs and Border Patrol. This had to be an inside job. This guy had probably ensured the two boxes made it through the CBP security. LAX was one of several locations that received international mail. Nearby, likely in an unassuming warehouse, there was probably a CBP setup to scan all incoming packages. I knew they had drug-detection equipment, but beyond that, I wasn't sure how the process went. Didn't matter right now.

"What does your daughter look like?" He smirked, rubbed his chin again.

This guy was a pervert. Not surprising that he knew Carter and Nixon. Maybe he'd visited their sex prison. "Look, I don't know…she's just a normal teenage girl."

"You got pictures?"

It was all I could do to not ram my foot between his legs, throw him onto the ground, and pound his face into oblivion.

"No pictures," I said with nothing behind it.

"You got a phone," he said, nodding at my hand. "So, you got pictures."

I took in a breath. "This isn't mine. It was given to me by the person who sent me here."

"What's his name?" he shot back.

Was this a test? "I don't know. He didn't tell me."

"What's he look like?"

"Couldn't see it. He had on a mask."

A slow smile split his lips. Something shined from his teeth. Braces? Gold? Again, it didn't matter. But it also made me wonder about the CBP hiring practices.

"Okay, well…" His eyes looked off into the distance, and he rubbed that chin again like it was some type of genie in a bottle. I wondered what he was conjuring up.

"So, can I just—"

"You ain't taking anything until I get my money."

Money? Carter never said a damn thing about a money exchange. Did it make sense that some type of currency would be used to pay for the product I was picking up? Yes. But Carter would have sent the money with me, or at least arranged for a wire transfer ahead of time. Unless Carter expected me to basically take it from this person, even if it meant a physical confrontation.

Shit!

Was this another reason I was chosen for this mission and not the Faulks? Carter might have thought that I could win a fight against this guy, if it came to that.

If it came to that? Surely, Carter knew the details. Was Carter trying to rob this guy of the product? Was this guy alone? Hell, he could whistle, and three other guys could show up in the back yard and pummel me into dust.

"I'm sorry," I said, trying to keep my voice even, "but I'm not aware of any type of money exchange. Perhaps you can call my contact in Las Vegas and discuss any financial details."

A single shake of the head. "You're smooth. Too smooth. It's like you've got all the answers."

Did that mean he wasn't expecting a money exchange? I couldn't read his exact intentions. Part of me wondered if he was just toying with me.

"I'm being transparent with you. I was told to do this one thing, and then—"

"I know, I know…then you get your daughter back. Whatever." He seemed bored with the topic now. I considered that good news.

He stepped back and pulled the door open. "Come on in. I've

got the boxes hidden in my room."

I paused a second. I didn't want to set him off again. I really had no choice—I had to go inside. I lumbered up two concrete steps and stepped into the kitchen. There was a lamp on in the corner. Lots of dishes stacked up in the sink. A single chair and table. Pretty sparse.

"I'll just be a second." He disappeared down a darkened hallway.

The refrigerator was making a constant buzzing sound—the model had to be from the previous century, or thereabouts. It was covered in scratches, like someone had gone crazy and taken a machete to it. My eyes surveyed the kitchen some more. I was tempted to look inside a drawer and find a knife I could stash in my pocket. If he caught me, though, he might go ape-shit.

I spotted some mail on the counter, so I shuffled one step to the right, and looked down to see a name: Grant Valdez. I assumed that was the CBP guy's name. I made a mental note to remember it. Eventually, once Erin and Becca were safe, I intended to take down this entire drug-prostitution ring. For now, though, nothing would divert my attention away from saving my daughter.

"Okay, here's the first box." He walked into the kitchen holding a taped-up corrugated box. He seemed to be straining a bit.

"Heavy?"

"They put fifty-pound weights in it, so it doesn't get flagged."

That verified the boxes had come from another country. But surely Grant wasn't the main cog in this operation. He was living in a glorified dump. Still, though, I wondered exactly what was in the box. I assumed it was drugs. Outside of curiosity—my natural response was to always ask questions and seek more information—I knew it didn't matter.

"I can open the trunk for you," I said, walking out the door.

We reached the car, and he set the box in the trunk.

"Just need that last box." I thought a second. "I'll just stay here by the trunk to make sure no one steals it. After all, it's worth a lot of money."

"Actually, I need your help," he said, backpedaling toward the open gate. "The contents of the other box fell out all over the floor. It might take a while for me to pick it all up. I don't want to be accused of stealing anything…if you know what I mean."

I just wanted to get the hell out of Gardena and start the drive back to Las Vegas. "Sure, okay."

We walked inside, and I followed him down the hall and into a bedroom. A lamp with no shade illuminated the room. The carpeting was shag—a puke green, no less. Next to a mattress with no frame, there was a wicker side table with a plate of food on it—some remnants of rice and a couple of pieces of leftover chicken.

"Where's the mess?"

An arm wrapped around my neck—I'd momentarily turned my back on Grant. His hold was tighter than I expected. I could hardly breathe. He used his other hand to grope my breast. I smacked at his hand. I could hear him laughing.

"Come on now," he said. "Fighting back is going to make this a lot less romantic."

I dug my nails into his arm—that had no effect. The lack of oxygen was numbing my brain. A wave of panic rushed over me. I rocked my body violently left and then right, but he seemed to be expecting it. He was agile and went with the motion.

My head felt like an overblown balloon—as if it might pop at any moment. Either that or I might pass out. Then what? He'd have his way with me, maybe worse. And Erin would never be saved. I tried to reach over my head and gouge his eyes, but he smacked my hands away. I was losing strength by the second. I stomped on his feet. Still he clung to me. I swung an elbow into his gut. He jerked back to avoid the full impact. It was like he knew my playbook.

"Let's just lie down on the bed, and you can rock my world," he said with a chuckle.

I'd underestimated Grant Valdez, and I was about to pay a dear price for it. But my thoughts—and I knew these might be my last lucid thoughts—went to Erin. She was experiencing something far worse than Grant Valdez. He was just one man. She was a scared child surrounded by deviants.

A second later, he slammed me down to the mattress, got on top me, and used his knees to hold down my arms. Most importantly, though, the pressure on my throat had been relieved. I gasped out a few breaths.

"Now, let's use that mouth for what God intended." He smiled while unbuckling his trousers.

I struggled to move my arms. There was a little give, but I didn't press it. Not until I had a plan.

He took off his shirt, threw it in the corner. "I'm going to get undressed. If you move from this position, I will beat the snot out of you. Your face won't be recognizable."

I didn't move.

"You doubt me?"

"No."

"Good. Because, just for your awareness, I was the LA Golden Gloves champ in the hundred-fifty-two-pound weight class. I knocked out twenty-four fighters in my amateur career." He held up a fist and popped it against his opposite hand.

I could feel the power. Damn, I'd really misjudged this guy.

He stood up on the mattress and lowered his pants.

"I'll take my own clothes off," I said.

"Now you're talking."

I shifted my legs and turned to sit on the edge of the bed.

"What the fuck do you think you're doing?" He grabbed my ponytail and jerked my head back.

I let out a squeal. "I'm just a little shy. Where do you expect me to go? I know you're faster and definitely a hell of a fighter. I'll do whatever you want, and then I'll leave."

He nodded. "Okay. Not very romantic, but you're treating this like a transaction. You go down on me, I give you the last box." He laughed mockingly, as if he'd just negotiated the greatest one-sided deal in the history of the world.

For whatever reason, my mind was hit with a slice of irony—I was in LA, the epicenter of the entertainment world, and ground zero for the secrets of so many men using their position of power to harass, assault, and rape so many women. And here I was, a so-called trained law-enforcement official, who was stupid enough to get herself in the same situation.

I started unbuttoning my shirt while my eyes darted around the room. I spotted a hard-soled shoe on the floor. I tried to picture myself lunging off the bed, grabbing the toe-end of the shoe, and then swinging the shoe and connecting with his jaw. Two problems. First, I wouldn't have a very good grip on the shoe, which meant I probably wouldn't have a lot of torque behind my swing. Second, with Grant being a boxer, he probably had a solid jaw. It would take a hell of a shot to even daze him.

I needed another plan.

"You're taking too long," he said in singsong mode. "Speaking of 'long,' I think you're going to need to channel your Watergate informant." He laughed at his sick "Deep Throat" joke.

I wasn't about to turn around. Not until I was forced to do so.

I thought my pounding heart might crack a rib. I was afraid, but more than anything I was fucking pissed! This maggot thought he had all the power over me…to service him in any way he saw fit. Fuck him!

In the midst of my disgust came a thoroughly simple idea. It was my one—maybe my only—chance to escape.

I jumped up and screamed, "Mouse, mouse, mouse!" I pointed at the floor while hopping up and down, feigning revulsion to something that didn't exist.

"Where?" Grant said, spinning around on the mattress.

"Over there, by the closet. Eeeww! I think I might vomit!" I said, lathering on the horror of seeing a mouse.

"I've got traps all over the house. How did he get through?" Grant leaped off the bed, pushed the box away from the front of the closet, and searched for the nonexistent mouse.

While he wasn't watching, I grabbed the fork off the plate and ran for the door.

"Hey, what the fuck, bitch!"

With his footsteps pounding just behind me, I cut right just outside of his room and pressed my back against the wall. I knew I'd have just one chance, just one swing of my arm. It was a zero-sum game—if I didn't hit the mark, he'd beat the shit out of me.

Just as I saw his knee emerge from the room, I whipped my arm around like I was hitting a top-spin forehand—with all the power of a Serena Williams, or back in my day, Steffi Graf.

The trajectory was perfect, and as I'd hoped, he wasn't expecting it, so his arms weren't raised. The fork skewered his left eye. He belted out a wail that probably had the dolphins in the Pacific Ocean in a tither. He reached up for the fork. I grabbed his shoulders for leverage, then cracked my foot off his groin. He made a sound like he had a punctured lung. His lone functional eye rolled to the back of his head, as blood drained down his face from his other eye.

I grabbed his arm, spun into the bedroom, and flipped him across the mattress. Slithering to the floor, he screamed like a prepubescent boy—maybe he didn't like the taste of his balls in the back of his throat. He curled up on the floor on the other side of the bed. I went over to the box, lowered my butt and legs, and pushed it through the house. Once at the back door, I shoved up my sleeves, picked up the fifty-pound box, and waddled to the trunk of the car.

Five minutes later, I passed Hustler Casino, thankful to put Gardena, California, in my rearview mirror.

Eleven

Ivy

Saul stuck his head in the bathroom just as I was trying to apply some mascara.

"Can I help you?" I asked, eyeing him through the reflection in the mirror.

"You stopped moving," he said with a smile on his face.

"Because I'm looking at you. I don't do this makeup thing very often, you know, so I have to focus."

He stepped into the bathroom and kissed the nape of my neck. Goose-bumps alert! I pressed my shoulder against his head. He then stepped behind me, held my hips, and gave me soft kisses from my shoulder to my ear.

"Oh my," I said. "Are you trying to recreate the scene we made in that St. Croix hotel?"

He didn't respond. Well, not verbally. Another part of him was very responsive. My entire body was tingling. "Stop teasing me," I said, halfway between a giggle and a dream state.

"Who said I'm teasing?"

I saw his eyes in the mirror over my shoulder as he ran his hands up my torso. My heart fluttered. This type of interaction used to scare me. Now, I leaned into it…so to speak.

"Saul, I thought we had this important Chamber of Commerce dinner to go to."

"The what?"

He was acting like a lion that hadn't been fed in a month. In reality, he'd been fed quite well—just last night, in fact.

"Okay…well, it's for your little law firm. So, I'm game if you're game." I dropped the mascara in the sink, turned around, and wrapped my arms around him. We kissed as though one of us had just escaped danger. That was my old life, though, when I'd spent far too much time trying to elude perverted deviants and killers. Ever since I'd opened my heart to Saul—not just on the surface but at a deeper level than I'd thought possible—I felt a joy and happiness about life. And, at the same time, there had been a dramatic decrease in run-ins with the miscreants of the world.

I'd read an article recently that basically said what you believe—what you surround yourself with—will be what you receive. After so many years of pushing people away, of finding countless reasons not to open up and give myself to another person, I was reaping the rewards of falling in love with Saul.

We shuffled into my bedroom and fell onto the bed, our lips and hands not losing a second of time. And then came the buzz.

"Whose phone is that?" I asked, coming up for air.

He snorted out a laugh.

"What?"

He looked at my lips, then used his forefinger to touch them. "I love your lips," he said.

My lipstick. "I think that means I look like a clown."

The buzz sound again. "Whose phone is that?" he asked this time, lifting his head off the bed.

We sat up. He reached for his phone, and I grabbed my purse from the bedside table. "Not my phone," he said, tossing it back on the table.

"What about the awards dinner? Aren't you up for Best New Law Firm?" I asked, fishing through my purse for my phone. He'd opened a one-man shop just over a year earlier and had done quite well for himself.

"We can make a dramatic late entrance." He started unzipping my little black dress. I was told by my friend Zahera that every girl needed a little black dress. Right now, Saul didn't agree with that notion.

"Got it."

Saul was strumming his fingers along my spine and kissing my neck. "Got what?" he murmured. Clearly, his mind was focused on planet ecstasy.

I was reading a text message from Stan, my detective friend with the San Antonio Police Department.

"Hmm," I said.

Saul sat up next to me. "Okay, I know when to take a hint." He winked at me and zipped up my dress. "Go ahead—tell me the sad story about one of your latest parent-clients whose sixteen-year-old child hasn't been seen since lunchtime."

"Funny." He was recalling a similar situation a while back when one panicked mother had called, begging me to do everything in my power to locate her "little darling." Her son happened to be a two-hundred-fifty-pound offensive tackle for the high-school football team. As it turned out, he'd skipped school to smoke weed with his fellow offensive lineman. I did get a thousand bucks out of the short-lived gig, but Saul said he hoped we would never become such helicopter parents. I tried not to remind him that his pushy mother flirted dangerously close to that line now, and he was thirty years old.

"Seriously," he said, standing up. "What's up with the text?"

I tapped a finger to my chin.

"I know that look, Ivy. Does this have to do with the Amber Alert?"

I shifted my eyes up to his. "Kind of."

"Kind of?"

"Okay, well…yes. Kind of."

He let out a chuckle.

"You know me, it's just hard to turn away."

"But I don't get the issue," he said, tucking his shirt in and adjusting his tie. "You saved the girl. The *Express-News* will probably write a nice article on your daring rescue, which will give ECHO a nice PR boost."

"I don't care about that stuff." More tapping against my chin.

He sat back down, put a hand on my knee. I turned my head and looked at him. He popped his eyebrows as his hand slowly moved up my thigh.

"You're so deprived," I said. "Or are you just hitting your sexual peak?"

He tapped my thigh and then stood up again. "Okay, I know you have something on your mind. You want to talk about it on the way to the dinner?"

I didn't respond.

"Oh, wait." He pointed at the phone. "Who texted you?"

"Stan. I'd asked him earlier if he could speak with the father to see if he would talk to me."

"Why would you even want to do that? Are you writing a book or something—what makes the criminal mind tick?"

"Not exactly."

He nodded. "You're in the mode."

"Sorry." I stood up and put a hand on his chest. "When the cops arrested him, the man didn't seem to be what I was expecting."

"You did say he looked like an average guy, wasn't all inked up with scars on his face and wearing a torn T-shirt. But you and I both know that could be a façade for what's really going on up here." He popped a finger to the side of his head.

"Maybe. Probably. But he also started saying how the little girl—I found out her name is Lila—would be in danger if given back to her mother. Stan's text says I can meet with this guy *if* I can get there in the next thirty minutes. I just want to hear him out. Is that so wrong?"

He kissed my cheek. "It's who you are, Ivy. One of the many reasons I love you."

"I'll meet you at your dinner. I promise to make it before they get to your award announcement."

He smacked my butt. "Do your thing, Ivy."

I smacked his butt in return.

I was gone before he could make another patented move on me.

Twelve

Alex

Thirty minutes after I left the home of Grant Valdez, I put in my mandatory hourly status call.

"I have the two boxes, and I'm in the car headed back to the compound."

Carter said, "Okay." An extra second of silence. "Good."

That brief pause made me wonder if he'd expected to receive this call from me. It was as though he knew that Valdez would attack me, hold me hostage, maybe kill me. Had this whole thing been a setup to lure me to Valdez's home so he could rape me? That didn't sound plausible. Back at the compound—and even before then, when they'd threatened to kill Erin to get me out to Vegas—it seemed like Carter and Nixon had a plan: use me to pick up their drugs. So, why had they sent me into Valdez's sex cave without any warning? Why, now, did Carter sound surprised to hear from me?

I waited an extra beat to see if Carter would ask me about Valdez. He didn't. I considered telling him how I was damn lucky to escape with my life and his two precious boxes, but I held back.

"Not sure what time I'll arrive," I said.

"Just continue calling in with your hourly status updates."

Click.

A deep sigh.

I put an elbow on the door and used a hand to prop up my head as I stared into a sea of red. Brake lights lit up the winding path of interstate traffic.

"The City of Angels," I said to myself, immediately seeing the irony in the name. You had to have wings and fly over this gridlock to have any hope of making decent time to get through the city traffic.

I'd had enough time to calm down some after my run-in with Grant Valdez. I was certain, though, that he wouldn't soon forget me. I just hoped it would scare him into changing his behavior.

"Yeah, good luck with that." I'd been talking to myself more and more since I'd essentially been shut off from the rest of the world. On the way to LA, I had this strange sense that someone was watching my every movement. Carter had told me not to contact anyone or he would harm Erin. That fear had kept me from reaching out to Brad, Jerry, or anyone else. Now, as I crawled through ever-thickening traffic, I began to question my judgment. It just didn't seem possible that a person could tail me through all this traffic into and now out of LA. I didn't doubt that Carter and Nixon were tracking my general movement through some type of GPS-tracker on the phone they'd given me or even on the Chrysler 300. Unless they'd contracted with a firm that had dispatched a fleet of drones, personal surveillance seemed unlikely.

I wondered if that should change my current approach. Brad was probably worried like hell about me. Maybe I could stop at a gas station and ask a random person to borrow a phone. If I shared with Brad what I'd actually experienced, though, wouldn't he worry even more? He'd probably try to talk me into getting Jerry involved and initiating some type of FBI raid on the compound. Part of me thought that was the prudent move. But I couldn't help but feel a nibble at the back of my mind. I had no idea who the men were behind the Carter and Nixon masks, or how far-reaching their operation was. Did they have contacts in law enforcement that allowed them to run their drug-sex business under the radar?

I knew that prostitution was legal in most of the Nevada counties, so that fact probably made it easier to get away with this illegal operation, and easier on whoever was helping to provide cover...local police, state police. Did it go any higher than that? Government officials or even federal officials stationed in Nevada?

There was no way for me to know. As isolated as I felt even amongst the millions of people bustling around LA, I decided to stay the course. I had what I came for: the two boxes of what I believed were drugs. My only question was what would happen once I drove into the compound and gave Carter and Nixon this so-called ransom? Would they hold up their end of the bargain and allow Erin and Becca to leave with me?

Squeezing the steering wheel, I took in a deep breath. My emotions had been driving nearly every decision up to this point. My FBI brain, though, was making a strong play right now.

"Will they hold up their end of the bargain and allow Erin and Becca to leave with me?"

Saying it out loud turned up my FBI radar. The answer wasn't clear cut, though. Carter and Nixon had hidden their faces for a reason—obviously, they didn't want me to identify them. But to whom? Before, I was thinking they were concerned about me giving their descriptions to law enforcement. But what if they were actually worried about me telling someone else?

Possibly Valdez?

The guy seemed like he was on a fast track to nowhere. Carter, on the other hand, had this air about him that made me think he swam in money. Probably all illegally acquired, but I doubt he'd ever worked a blue-collar job in his life.

Was there someone else on this trek that I'd yet to encounter, someone to whom they thought I might spill the beans? It was possible. But once I made it back to the compound, what use did they have for me? Did they think I would take the girls, say "thank you," and then simply move on with my life? They knew I worked for the FBI. And once I had the girls in safe custody, they had to know that I'd send in the cavalry. Unless…unless they intended on holding something over my head. A new threat that would keep my mouth shut.

I drummed my fingers on the steering wheel column and contemplated how I should deal with this dilemma. My initial thought? I was screwed either way. Carter and Nixon probably knew I wanted my Erin back even more than they wanted their drugs. They had the upper hand. I couldn't play hardball. As I juggled all the possibilities, it was if a steel plate were forming in my neck. I rubbed it vigorously, but I knew it would do no good. Brad had his ways of relieving my tension—what I would give to feel that kind of normalcy again. But he wasn't around.

No one was.

Thirteen

Ivy

The father's name was Gerald Bailey. Stan had told me that much when I arrived at the police department that also housed a jail for those waiting to be arraigned. As Stan accompanied me to an interrogation room, he gave me the eye.

"What?" I said.

"You're dressed like a woman."

My little black dress.

Stan wasn't ogling. He, like most people not named Saul, typically saw me in clothes that blended in with the crowd. Plain-Jane. Vanilla. Whatever you want to call it. Stan was like an older brother to me, a big lovable bear. Check that. He *used* to be a big bear, eating everything his paws touched—donuts and candy bars were two of his favorites. But after losing his arm to a homicidal maniac—courtesy of my most zealous past demon—he took the challenge laid down by his cousin Nick, an FBI agent out of the Boston office. They would race each other in the Boston Marathon, with the winner carrying the ultimate bragging rights. Stan first had to drop about eighty pounds. He changed his diet, ran twice a day, sometimes with me. But he was fiercely driven by the need to beat his cousin in the race.

During the marathon, however, a series of bombs were detonated. Stan escaped injury, but Nick wasn't as lucky. After two surgeries, his life had hung in the balance for a couple of days. Stan stayed at his bedside almost the entire time. Nick survived, and from what I heard, he'd been recuperating nicely, eager to rejoin his partner, Alex Troutt, at the FBI. I'd worked with them both a while ago. Nick and Alex were good people, dedicated law-enforcement officers who weren't afraid to push things beyond the bureaucratic norm if it helped reach the investigative goal.

"Did I tell you that Bailey—when I brought up your name—actually said he wanted to meet with you? Kind of surprised me, honestly, given you're the one who chased him down. So that's why this meeting is happening. His lawyer advised him against meeting with you, but Bailey was hell-bent on it."

Interesting.

During the rest of the walk to the interrogation room, Stan talked about his wife Bev and their son. Ethan had autism. It had taken a toll on the family, but I'd also seen the three of them share some special moments, although most were short-lived. Stan called them snapshots because they happened so quickly. But he told me he'd learned to treasure those moments, adding, "I could have never predicted any of this. Didn't think it would happen to me. But after I stopped feeling sorry for myself, I realized that life's greatest challenges can also be life's greatest rewards. You just have to keep your eyes open or you'll miss them."

Stan opened the door to the room. Bailey was already in his seat. He was handcuffed to a metal railing on top of a table that was bolted to the floor. It seemed like overkill, but I kept my mouth shut. A uniformed officer stood in the corner. He gave me a cordial nod.

"If I want to get home before midnight, I need to go knock out some work at my desk," Stan said, using his prosthetic arm to motion over his shoulder. "The officer, here, will take Bailey back to his cell once you're done. You've got fifteen minutes."

"Thanks." I turned and suddenly felt a bit conspicuous about my attire. Not because of Bailey. But because of the officer, who kept shifting his eyes to me. I wasn't used to the Zahera treatment—my dear friend was a goddess. In my pre-Saul days, whenever she and I went out, every pair of eyes devoured her. I'd served as nothing more than her interesting sidekick, which had been fine by me.

I ignored the cop and sat down.

"Thank you for taking the time to come and speak with me." Bailey sat a little taller in his chair. Outside of his county-issued orange jumpsuit, he looked like a regular guy. Different than when I'd seen him jumping out of his car, covered in sweat, his face full of fear and rage. Right now, he seemed calm. Then I noticed that he was wringing his hands, probably trying his hardest to contain his anxiety.

"Why did you do it, Mr. Bailey?"

"Please call me Gerald."

"Okay. Gerald. Why did you kidnap Lila, and what did you intend to do to her?"

"Wow, you don't waste any time, do ya?"

The questions had spilled from my lips without any effort. I'd dealt with men like Gerald Bailey more times than I could count. I lifted my hands and let them drop to the table. "I don't want to waste my time listening to you justify the kidnapping of a little girl who was obviously very scared."

He tried bringing his arm to his chest, but his cuffed wrist stopped that movement. He shook his head. "You've got to know that I would never do anything to Lila. That little girl is…" He looked off into the distance. His dark eyes became glassy. He gulped in a breath and then turned back to me. "I love Lila. She's a jewel. But it's because I love her so much that I did what I did."

I crossed my legs. "Here we go." Why had I wanted to speak with this guy?

"Hold on a second. Hear me out."

"I'm listening…at least as long as I can stand it in the few minutes we have."

"I'm not a perfect person, Ms. Nash."

Ms. Nash? Sounded matronly. "You can call me Ivy."

"Ivy, okay. Well, I know I'm not a perfect husband or even the perfect father. But I do love my girls. Every family member, every friend will tell you that."

I was sure that could be verified. I motioned with my hand for him to continue.

"Look, you're the woman who kept me from getting away. Most guys would want to bust you up. But here I am talking to you…of my own volition. Want to know why?"

"Why?"

"Because I looked you up. Well, I had my lawyer do it. He told me you own a PI firm that specializes in helping kids who are in bad situations. ECHO, right?"

"Gerald, this is really up to the courts now. If you convinced the police that Lila is truly in danger—and I'd like to hear why you think that—Child Protective Services will likely open a case and go visit the home."

I did an internal eye roll. CPS in the state of Texas was an absolute joke. I knew…because I'd once worked there. I could fill a spreadsheet with a list of things on how that agency let down so many kids. Their ineptitude had led to countless children being abused, raped, even murdered. When I couldn't take any more of their gross negligence, I'd left and created

ECHO. Cristina and I had grown a nice little business, but we didn't hide behind a bunch of bureaucratic rules. A child's safety always came first, even when that went against the requests of paying clients.

"Jill is an addict," he said, staring me in the eye.

"Your wife?"

He nodded, closed his eyes for a brief moment. "I used to have a lot of empathy for her. I tried to help her. Put her in rehab a half dozen times. Every time, though, she'd come out and swear she was clean. Then, usually within a few weeks, I'd start seeing the signs. I was afraid to go to frickin' work, not sure what condition she'd be in when I got home."

"Where do you work?"

"Not sure I'll still have a job after all this, but I do IT project management at a firm called PMI."

Not your typical Amber Alert perpetrator. "Tell me more about your wife's issue."

"We used to be happy. She was a nurse. I did my PM gig. We made decent money, I guess. One day I found pills in the medicine cabinet that weren't prescribed to either one of us. I asked her about it, and she said she had one of the doctors at her hospital give her something for a sore back. I thought nothing of it. Well, a few weeks go by, and I see another bottle, this one filled to the top. I didn't say anything. I checked the bottle a few days later, and it was almost empty. That's when I started connecting the dots."

"The dots. What am I missing?"

"She'd changed. She was always sick to her stomach, lost a lot of weight, had huge mood swings. She looks gaunt, you know, like she has two black eyes."

"And you had nothing to do with those black eyes?"

He made a scoffing noise. "I know I'm wearing this orange

get-up, and I'm in handcuffs, but this isn't me. I don't break the law. Ever. I sure as hell wouldn't hit a woman."

"What about your daughter?"

"Harm my daughter? You think I would harm my daughter?" His eyes fluttered as I saw his intensity skyrocket.

"Calm down. I'm just asking a question. You wanted me here."

He huffed out a breath. "I was raised by two good parents who taught me to treat everyone with respect, starting with women."

"Very noble of you."

"You're skeptical. I can understand why. But you have to believe that my wife is an addict. I'm telling you that she's a different woman than when I married her." He used his shoulder to rub his face. "If you don't believe me on that point, then I guess you'll never believe anything else I say."

Gerald suddenly looked like he'd aged another ten years. Creases around his eyes appeared deep enough to hold a coin. I shifted in my seat, allowing my mind to walk through everything he'd shared up to now.

"What's her drug of choice?" I asked.

"Fentanyl."

One of the most popular and lethal opioids that had been tearing a deadly swath across the country. "Okay, let's assume I agree that your wife has a severe addiction issue."

He put his palms flat on the table and released a pocketful of air. "Okay. Good."

"That being said, you still haven't told me why you lost it and ran off with your child. And, more importantly, why she would call the police on you if you've done nothing wrong."

"Five more minutes," the cop said from the back of the room.

I gave him a quick nod, then looked to Gerald. "Well?"

"Being married to an addict is like…I don't know." He shook his head. "It's like being chained to the Tasmanian Devil. She's all over the place, so needy at times, so hateful at other times. It's fucking exhausting." He cleared his throat. "Pardon my language."

"Continue," I said.

"So, this morning her paranoia was at a level ten, I'm telling you. She was all over the place, ranting and raving about one thing or another, usually ending with me. She finally went back to take a nap. So, I stayed home from work and played with our youngest, Lila."

"You have an oldest?"

He smacked his hands on the table. "That's what I *really* want to talk to you about."

I'd recalled his last statement before the cops stuffed him in the police car. *"You can't take her back to her mother. Both of my daughters are…"* That statement had lingered in my mind. It was why I'd, ultimately, called up Stan, hoping to understand what was really going on. Well, that and something about Gerald Bailey didn't seem to fit the stereotype of a child kidnapper. I wasn't sure if my intuition was throwing up false flags. Now, I was having even more doubts.

"Keep going. This morning you were playing with Lila and…?"

He nodded twice. "A guy knocks on our door. I open it, and he says he wants his damn money. I don't know what the hell he's talking about. We don't typically carry much debt. If so, it's paying off credit cards, like most people. I thought he was a quack—kind of looked like it too—so I start shutting the door on him. That asshole actually stuck his foot in the door, wouldn't let me shut it. He shoved the door open and said if he didn't get his five grand then something might happen to someone I cared about. He shifted his bloodshot eyes over to my daughter. I grabbed him and..." Gerald stopped, looked toward the cop over his shoulder.

"You might as well tell me everything, Gerald. If you're really telling the truth, then it shouldn't matter."

He let out a shaky breath. "I just told the guy that he better not come around the house anymore. And if he got near my daughter, I'd be forced to call the cops or, if needed, beat the shit out of him." He shook his head, muttered something.

"Care to share?"

"Oh, the guy was so cocky, so brazen. He chuckled and walked off to his car. I just stood there, defiant-like. When he got in the car, he waved a gun where I could see it, and then yelled that he'd be back in an hour. And that I might want to talk to my wife and find out how serious he can be."

Gerald's breathing picked up. He kept trying to rub his face, though he couldn't because of the cuffs. His anxiety was difficult to watch.

"It's time for me to take him back to his cell," the cop said, walking toward the table.

I held up a hand. "Please hold off. We just need another five minutes."

"Ms. Nash, I've been told to give you fifteen minutes. I even gave you a five-minute warning."

"Two minutes, then. That's all I'm asking for."

His eyes gave me the once-over. It made me more than a little uncomfortable. Did he think I was going to maybe flash him a breast just to get him to cooperate? He obviously didn't know me very well, if that were the case.

"Okay," he finally said. "Two minutes." He found his spot back in the corner.

"Talk, Gerald," I said.

"So, I go wake up Jill and confront her about this guy who's threatened to harm Lila. She frickin' loses it. Says she doesn't need my permission to do anything. It was making no sense. She hasn't made sense in a long time, but this...this was different." He poked his finger into the table. "We were talking about the safety of Lila. Isn't protecting your child against bad people the most fundamental part of being a parent?"

I nodded, motioned with my hand for him to keep talking. I knew the cop was counting seconds.

"Jill and I started fighting—I didn't back down this time. She wouldn't tell me who this guy was, but I flat-out accused her that she owed money to her dealer. She told me I was full of it, but I knew she was lying. She said I was the one on drugs if I thought she'd interact with someone who might harm Lila. She was belligerent. I could see that she was in full-on 'lie mode.' I couldn't trust a word that came out of her mouth."

"So you took Lila?"

He nodded. "Didn't even know where I was going. Just knew I couldn't keep her there."

"Why didn't you call the cops?"

He moved his hands enough to clang the cuffs against the metal bar. "I don't know. I guess I thought that Jill would lie her way out of it. And if this drug dealer didn't come back in one hour, he'd come back five hours later, after the cops left, or the next day. I couldn't trust anyone."

The cop walked over and started to unlock Gerald's cuffs.

"Quickly," I said. "Tell me about your other child."

"Angel is fifteen. About two weeks ago, when I was out of town on a consulting gig, Jill shipped her off to her sister's place. Said she needed a break from the pressure at school. I went along with it initially, but after a few days, I called out there, and Jill's sister, Jenny, said Angel had made a new friend and wasn't at the house. I tried over and over again to reach Angel, but she was never around."

The cop pulled Gerald up to a standing position.

"Angel is a bit of a pistol, but I could never see her not talking to me for two weeks. It's just not her."

The cop walked Gerald to the door.

"What are you saying, Gerald?"

Tears streamed down his face. "After what happened this morning, I'm worried that Jill did something…maybe gave Angel to this drug dealer as part of paying off her debt, and then got her sister to cover for her. Will you try to find her? Please. No one believes me."

"I'll do what I can."

He was ushered out of the room. I sat in silence for a few minutes and pondered if I should believe Gerald Bailey.

Fourteen

Alex

I finally reached the north side of LA, saw a sign for Pasadena to the west, but I headed east on the 210—I'd been brainwashed into using "the." I hit the 15 and traversed north, leaving the glow of the big city lights behind me.

As I made my way across the state, I thought more about my options with Carter and Nixon and the drugs in the back of my car. I knew they'd balk at an in-your-face threat—something like "give me the girls or I toss the drugs down a drain." In fact, they might react violently against the girls. But what if something kept me from arriving at the compound? A flat tire, or some type of car trouble? They'd either be forced to bring the girls to me, or if one of them came alone, I felt reasonably confident I could take him. Of course, if more than one former president came to pick me up, then I was screwed.

Too many ways to get screwed in this deal. No option was perfect, nor without some risk. That was the way all ops went. Ultimately, I'd have to rely on my experience and my instinct. And maybe a little bit of luck.

A flash of light made me blink. I checked my rearview. A car was flashing its brights. But it was the swirling red and blue lights on top of the car that made my breath hitch.

I had to think quickly. I was about to pass an exit, but I swerved right just before I ran into a metal barricade. I purposely didn't hit the gas—I didn't want the officer to think I was running from him. The frontage road was even darker than the interstate. We were in the mountains. I recalled seeing a sign for Mountain Pass. As I slowed the car, I spotted a dirt road off to the right. I pulled to a stop just near it, where weeds and chiseled boulders camouflaged the opening.

Blood flooded my brain. I wasn't exactly sure how to handle this. I might be the victim in this fucked-up ransom mission, but to a cop, I was a woman driving an old car across the mountains headed straight for Sin City, and in the trunk were two boxes of drugs. Over time, I'd probably be able to talk my way out of it—after he arrested me, brought me back to his station, and then put in a few calls. It might be well into the next day before everything got ironed out. How many hourly status calls would I miss? More importantly, how many could I afford to miss before Carter and Nixon retaliated against Erin and Becca?

I watched in my side mirror as a cop walked toward my car. It was a male, that much I could see. "Brad…I'm doing this for Erin and Becca," I said to myself. I unhooked my bra, slipped it through my sleeve, and then unbuttoned my shirt to my navel. Jennifer Lopez had nothing on me. I just had to hope this guy was straight and had a little bit of Grant Valdez in him.

I clicked the window button as he walked up and shined a flashlight in my face. I arched my back to provide the best cleavage shot.

"Evening officer." I smiled, batting my lashes.

Through the glare, I could see the man reset his hat. The muscles in his forearms rippled. He leaned down to where I could see his face. His eyes went right to my chest.

Bingo.

"I'm Officer Massey." He paused and looked around the inside of the car.

"I hope you're having a great night. Me? I'm just taking a leisurely drive to Las Vegas. I have a friend there, and we're going to have some fun."

He nodded, his eyes back on my chest. He seemed to be contemplating his next move. If he asked for my driver's license, I was screwed. The phrase of the day, apparently.

I giggled.

"Have you been drinking, miss?"

"Oh God, no. I had an uncle who died after being hit by a drunken driver. That's the last thing I would do. I'm just thinking about what me and my friend are planning to do once I get to Vegas."

He had his hands on his knees now. He looked back to his car and then to me. "And what's that?"

"We're planning on going to one of those amateur strip clubs and just letting it all loose. The full monty." I giggled for a second. Then, I stopped suddenly and put a hand to my face.

"What's wrong?" he asked.

I sniffled and conjured up tears. "It's nothing...well, I guess it's kind of something."

"If you want, I can call a female officer to the scene. We've been trained in dealing with people who are in emotional distress."

Was this guy that thick-headed?

I reached out and touched his hand for a brief moment. "It's not that. I'm just..." I lowered my head, then took in a deep breath that expanded my chest. When I looked up, I caught his eyes boring holes into my chest. He was actually licking his lips.

"I just found out my husband was cheating on me."

"Oh…I'm, uh…sorry."

"Thank you. But I feel like such an idiot. I saw that he'd been direct-messaging someone on Facebook. I just didn't know it was an old high-school girlfriend of his."

"I see."

"You're probably wondering how I know all this. Well, I walked in on them three hours ago, humping each other like two dogs in heat." More sniffles and tears.

He handed me a tissue, and I wiped my face.

"I'm so sorry," he said.

"It's okay. I'll be all right. He's cheated on me five other times in our marriage. I was an ignorant fool. But now I'm going to get mine. I'm going to Vegas, and the first stud I see, I'm going to get laid."

I could see his Adam's apple bob as he swallowed hard. I gave him a very obvious once-over. "What's your name?"

"I told you. Officer Massey."

"No, your first name."

"Bruce."

"Bruce," I said, gently biting my lower lip. "Well, my asshat husband will eventually feel my wrath. But right now…seriously, all I want to do is feel your rod."

His eyes got wide. He looked back to his car. "I'll be back in a second."

He scampered back to his car and leaned in. The lights went off. He then ran up to my car and slipped into the passenger seat. He wasn't wearing his hat any longer. His big ears looked like they could help him take flight. I tried not to chuckle.

"Take a right down this dirt road before anyone sees us," he said.

I turned on the car and followed his directions. I stopped about a half mile down, put the car in park, and dove on top of him. I pretended to be pawing at his shirt as he kissed on my chest. He was like a high-school kid, so single-minded that he had no idea what was going on around him. Before he could spit or wind his watch, I'd unsnapped the button of his holster, pulled out his pistol, and jumped back into the driver's seat.

"What the hell you doing, lady?" He slowly raised his arms. Then, he began to whimper. "Are you going to kill me and leave me for dead in the middle of nowhere until the vultures eat my carcass?"

"You have an active imagination, Bruce."

"Then what is this all about? I thought you were into me." He sounded like a whiny teenager.

I shook my head as I buttoned my shirt with my free hand. "You're pretty gullible, Bruce."

"Are you going to steal my money? I only have twenty bucks on me. I guess you can have my credit cards, but my wife will have my ass if I lose those."

"Bruce, you're not wearing a ring."

"You noticed." His chin dropped to his chest.

"Cheer up, Bruce. I'm not going to kill you or steal your money."

"Then what is this all about?"

"Give me the keys to your car."

"Why?"

I snapped my fingers, and he quickly produced the keys and put them in my hand.

"Okay, now your handcuffs."

"My handcuffs?"

"Are you hard of hearing?"

He looked at the gun.

I said, "I'm a trained professional. I know how to use this gun." Of course, he wasn't aware I had no intention of firing the weapon. It was all about power. Right now, I was wielding it so I could hopefully give myself a chance to save my daughter and her friend.

The whining had stopped, and I could see his mental gears were beginning to crank a bit. "This is something much bigger than taking me, isn't it?"

"You'll eventually find out what's going on. For right now, I need you to cooperate. So, you either trust me and do as I ask, or I'll be forced to put a bullet in your kneecap."

He huffed out a breath and set the cuffs on the seat.

"The keys to your handcuffs, please."

He produced them as well, and I put everything he'd given me on the floorboard in front of me. Then, I paused a second and re-thought my plan.

I grabbed the handcuffs and got out of the car, walked around to the other side, and opened his door. "Get out."

"Why?"

"Just get out."

"Please tell me what's going on? I'm sure I can help."

Yeah, right. "Bruce. I don't have much time. Get out of the fucking car."

He did as I said, and I shut the door. "Take off your clothes, down to your underwear."

"What the hell is this all about?"

He was confused, probably scared. I hated it more than he did, truth be told. But I couldn't stop now. "Not your concern. Take off your clothes and throw them behind the rocks over there," I said, motioning with my head.

He did it, and I didn't bother looking. "Get in the back seat."

He turned his palms to the dark sky, opened his mouth like he might say something, but shut his mouth and got in the car. I gave him the handcuffs. "Cuff yourself to the headrest."

"Seriously? What are you going to do to me?"

"Stop asking questions. Just do it." My voice had some steel to it, and he quickly complied with my request.

I knew he probably had the strength to pull the headrest off the seat, but it would take some effort. During those few seconds, I'd have enough time to grab the gun and, if necessary, shoot him. Or maybe I'd shoot and miss—to simply scare the shit out of him. Whatever was needed at this point.

He followed my instructions. I shut the back door, then walked around the car, slipped into the driver's seat, and started up the Chrysler.

"Are you going to tell me where you're taking me? I mean, I thought you said this wasn't about me."

I put the car in drive and started retracing my path down the dirt road toward the interstate.

"So now you're not talking to me," he said, shaking his head. I could hear him muttering something, but I couldn't pick it up. Probably cussing me out or regretting taking the bait I'd thrown him.

I reached the frontage road and spotted Bruce's police car. I considered getting in and moving it out of sight, but I didn't want to waste any more time. I made my way onto the interstate and continued my same path, moving east on the 15.

After traveling a couple of miles, I caught Bruce grasping the headrest with his hand. I held the gun up so he could see it. "Don't be a bad boy, Bruce. Bad boys will get punished. This is your last warning."

He dropped his head between his arms. "You were lying to me earlier, weren't you?"

I didn't respond.

"You're going to kill me. Or maybe you have some place in the middle of nowhere, and you're going to torture me because I jumped at the chance to have sex with you. It's all because I'm married, right?"

I was going to respond, but then he said, "Wait—Melody hired you, didn't she? Crap. I actually love that woman, but I just can't help myself sometimes."

Men. I wondered if my deceased husband, Mark, ever felt any remorse for his philandering. I wiped that from my thoughts. I traveled five more miles and found another exit that seemed to go nowhere. I took it and crawled along the dark frontage road. "There," I said out loud. I took a right turn down a dirt road. After about a mile, the terrain became rocky. I went another half mile or so and then stopped the car.

With the gun in my free hand, I opened Bruce's door and handed him the key to the handcuffs. "Unlock the cuffs."

He did. Then I motioned for him to get out of the car. He held the cuffs and the key in front of him. I took the keys back and put them in my pocket. "Re-cuff your hands together."

"So, you are some psycho bitch."

"Maybe. Just do it."

He did it. "You're going to kill me, aren't you? You're going to make me pay for almost cheating on my wife. How do you know I would have followed through with it?"

"Bruce, stop putting up a legal defense here. We both know you'd already crossed the line. If I were you, I'd do some serious thinking while you're out here all alone."

"What do you mean?"

"I mean it's time to grow up and be a real man."

He looked away for a second. Maybe he was pondering what that meant.

"Start walking." I motioned for him to continue down the dirt-and-rock road, away from the interstate.

"Walk where?"

"Hold on. First, take off your underwear and throw them in the back seat."

"You want them as some type of trophy? This is fucked up."

"In a lot more ways than you realize. Just do it, Bruce."

Again, he complied.

"Okay, now start walking."

He shuffled away for about twenty feet and then said, "You going to shoot me in the back?"

"Keep walking, Bruce. Everything will be fine as long as you keep walking."

"So you're going to leave me out here? There are coyotes, you know."

"I'm confident you can defend yourself."

"So you're just going to drive off?"

"Eventually. But I might come back to make sure you're not walking back to the interstate." I imagined how that would look to drivers, seeing a naked man in handcuffs waving at them from the side of the highway. I knew, eventually, he'd make his way back to the police station. From there, I wasn't sure if Bruce would relay the true story. It might be too embarrassing for him to reveal. But by then, I would hopefully be in Vegas and have the girls with me.

I waited until I could barely see him in the distance. "Good luck, Bruce," I shouted. "Remember, think about what you need to do to become a good man, a good husband."

"Who are you—the Ghost of Christmas Past?"

I didn't bother responding. I motored away with Bruce's gun in my car. We'd have to see if this Scrooge was going to have to kill someone to get her daughter back.

Fifteen

Ivy

I jogged so fast through the massive corridor inside the San Antonio Convention Center, I literally ran out of one of my heels. I jumped back and tried to put it on while moving. It wasn't working.

A man, who was carrying a tray of used dishes, stopped next to me. "Are you here for the—"

"Yes, yes. Tell me I'm not too late."

His eyes drifted to the ceiling for a moment. "Okay, you're not too late."

I finally got my shoe on. "Are you just telling me that?"

He shrugged. "I just told you what you wanted to hear. You can see for yourself."

Dammit. I hopped twice, attempting to slip my shoe back on—I didn't want Saul to think I'd put my work over him. I'd told him I would make it in time.

Maybe I missed the dinner but hopefully not the awards.

A rush of positive energy flowed through me. I leaned over, took off my other heel, and jogged to the last door on the left side. I opened it just as people came streaming out. Lots of chuckles and back-slaps, everyone was talking. A few of the men had loosened their ties. I saw two women make a beeline toward the restrooms. It was obvious, though, that the whole banquet had ended. I tried to push my way through, but it was like swimming—flailing, actually—upstream. I say that only because I can't swim. Another story for another day.

I was elbowed and bumped—not on purpose, of course. People were in their own worlds. I then spotted a woman carrying a crystal award. She was gleaming with pride. A man, probably her husband, leaned in and kissed her cheek, adding, "I'm so proud of you. I knew you could make this business work. You're my hero." She put a hand to the side of his face, stretched her smile even wider, and they walked past me.

Sigh.

The number of people was endless. Who knew the annual Chamber of Commerce Awards Banquet was so popular? Not me. Frustrated I couldn't find Saul, I climbed onto a chair and rotated until I spotted him. He was talking to two men. He was laughing while... Wait a second. I blinked, refocused my sights. He was holding one of those crystal awards.

Double dammit!

Jumping off the chair, I was both ecstatic and disheartened. Could someone actually feel both emotions at the same time?

I pushed my way through the loiterers and practically tackled Saul. "Congratulations!" I said, giving him a wet kiss on the cheek.

"Oh, hey," he said.

I grabbed the trophy out of his hand. "You could lift weights with this sucker."

"Ivy—"

"I'm so sorry I missed your big moment. Lots to catch you up on, but I was here in spirit."

I could feel the eyes of the other men. My little black dress again? They introduced themselves. They had the same last name. They looked very similar—thick, curly hair, same height and build. "You guys are twins?"

"They are," Saul said. "And I was just congratulating them for winning the award for Best New Law Firm."

I cleared my throat, giving my brain an extra second to play catchup. Yep, I confirmed it. I was a complete fucking moron.

"Sorry," I said, inadvertently making it sound like a question.

"It's okay," the twin on the left said. "Hey, Saul's got us beat. Neither of us has a beautiful woman running in here to congratulate us."

"Yeah," said the one on the right. "We're married to our jobs. That's probably how we won this award." He looked at his brother. "We need to get a life, man."

I handed back the trophy and the twins walked off.

"Tell me I didn't completely embarrass you after missing the banquet that I told you I wouldn't miss," I said, putting a hand to my forehead.

Saul wrapped his arm around my waist. "Just knowing you care means a lot." He leaned in and kissed my cheek.

"If they gave out an award for Worst Girlfriend, I would have won by a unanimous vote. Damn, I'm sorry, Saul. When I saw you holding the award, I was happy-sad."

He looked perplexed.

"Happy that you won, sad that I wasn't here."

A slow nod.

"And then I double the mistake by acting like an idiot in front of the twins."

"Eh. They basically threw it in my face, kind of forcing me to hold their great award."

"Assholes," I said, glancing over my shoulder. "Who needs them?"

"Who needs that stupid award, either?" Saul said, jumping on my bandwagon.

I took him in my arms and gave him a big smooch. I could hear a few *ooh*s and *ahh*s from people walking by. I paid them no attention.

A few seconds later, we finished our kiss. "Is this the same timid Ivy Nash I met when I ran into you at a drink machine?" he asked.

"Technically, yes. But do you recall asking me out at the same time you were handing me papers stating that I was being sued by your client?"

"Not really my client. *Ross's* client. Ross being the asshole I used to work for."

"How could I forget?"

I hooked my arm around his, and we strolled out of the banquet hall, mixing in with the horde of banquet attendees.

"So, how did it go with the kidnapper?" he asked.

"You sure you want me to spoil your night?"

"What night? I lost, remember. Besides, this glitzy stuff doesn't really matter. Well, then again, I could have used the award as a great PR tool, maybe put a picture of me on a few billboards holding the crystal trophy…"

I knew he was kidding. I goosed his ribs, and he jerked his elbow. I could feel the air of his arm swooshing by as it barely avoided ramming my nose. "Wow, I almost thought that was payback for me missing your big night," I said.

"Very funny. So, give me the scoop."

I did. It took so long to share the Gerald Bailey story, we'd trudged through the convention center and made it all the way to the back of the parking garage. When I finished, he didn't say anything. He just looked out across the city. The San Antonio skyline wasn't spectacular by any means, but it was on the rise.

"What do you think?" I asked.

"I was going to ask you the same thing," he said.

"What do you mean?"

"You think Gerald is telling the truth?"

I pursed my lips. "It's hard to say. Maybe some of it. Maybe most of it. I don't know. I've been going back and forth ever since he left the interrogation room. He certainly doesn't seem like a guy who would kidnap or harm his child."

"From what you said, though, he painted his wife as a pretty horrible person."

"The way he said it, though… I don't know. I sensed that he was breaking apart inside. The whole thing—his wife's addiction, her crazy behavior, his fear for his daughter, that crazy guy who showed up at the house. And then, of course, there's his other daughter who's supposedly living out in California. Or not. I mean, if you could have seen his face…"

He turned and looked at me. "You really think that a nurse—"

"*Former* nurse. And don't be fooled by her job, Saul. Gerald works in IT. He didn't look like your typical Amber Alert culprit."

"Right, don't judge a book by its cover. I get it. I just know that some domestic issues are so…"

"Complicated?"

"Beyond complicated. Both parties claim ownership to one hundred percent of the truth, and usually both are lying, at least a bit. They want the other person to look as bad as possible while making themselves look like white knights. It's all a precursor to a big custody battle. And some of these people can really put on a show."

I smacked his butt, just to get his attention.

"Hey, what's that for?"

"I've been around too, you know."

"You're right. I'm not questioning your judgment. Just sharing what I've seen. I represent men and women, and at times, the whole thing sickens me, to see people who supposedly were in love going after each other."

I didn't respond.

"But you think this is different."

I nodded. "Mostly. I just know if I ignore it, then what if it's true? What if that little girl is in danger? And what about his other daughter, Angel? God knows what could be going on in California."

"You're going to visit the mom, aren't you?"

I smirked.

"You were going to go before you brought it up to me."

"Maybe. I just needed to talk it out."

"Glad I'm a good sounding board, anyway."

"Oh, you're good for more than that."

He leaned in for a kiss. Before his lips landed, I opened my car door. "You've got your own car. First one home gets dibs."

He stood there with his arms open. "Dibs on what?"

"Exactly."

Sixteen

Alex

With the golden glow of dawn nipping at the horizon, I drove the car toward the compound. I planned to do a single drive-by, find a place about five miles out where I could park my car, and then put in the call to Carter.

After leaving Officer Bruce Massey naked and walking in the wilderness, I'd been fortunate to make the last leg of this trip without incident. I'd even passed two police cars, and while anxiety gripped my insides each time, they drove by and never paid me any attention.

My guess was that Bruce might have walked all the way back to where he'd removed his clothes, about a six-mile hike. Once there, he probably concocted some story to tell his superiors. I assumed most of it was embellished, maybe something like, *"I was kidnapped by two men who were walking along the frontage road. They threatened me with my own gun, put a bag over my head, and left me in the middle of nowhere."* He might have even trashed his precious credit cards just to make the story more believable. Anything to save face. While it might have been the greatest life lesson for him, I'm just glad it had worked for me and my situation.

The compound was located off a side road from a main highway in the middle of Nye County, about fifty miles northeast of Las Vegas. I shut off my phone as I neared the location—thinking that if they were tracking my location using the GPS on my phone, it wouldn't be too alarming for the signal to stop for a couple of minutes. I turned off my headlights as I took a right down the side road and crept along the gravel-and-dirt path. I pulled to a stop around a bend, my car still hidden behind a small hill of rocks. I got out and walked the last few feet until I reached the rocks, and then poked my head around the side.

While the place was mostly hidden by the fence and grassy knoll in front, when I'd left the compound yesterday, there had been several trucks and SUVs on the long driveway to the side of it. Right now, though, I didn't see a single one. None. Nada.

I felt a prick at the base of my skull as fear rippled through my extremities. Had Carter and Nixon taken Erin, Becca, and the whole operation to some other location?

Please tell me they're still here. Please tell me this mission wasn't just a sick joke.

I swallowed back some bile and moved in closer. Thankful it was still mostly dark, I stayed low to the ground, moving from one rock formation to the next. About sixty seconds later, I peered around the fence into the main yard in front of the building. I saw no lights on, no people, and no cars. No cars meant *no customers.* If they had no customers, then they weren't making money. If nothing else, I knew that Carter and Nixon were all about making money, the laws—moral and otherwise—be damned.

I jogged back to my car, got in, and drove off, thinking about what I should do next. Was now the time to call Jerry and assign about fifty agents to the case? It would take some time, maybe most of the day, since neither Jerry—as far as I knew—nor I had any local FBI contacts. We'd have to follow protocol, and FBI protocol can take a long time. Too damn long. On top of the timing issue, it was a life-or-death issue. If Carter and Nixon had the girls stashed away at another location—maybe taking extra precaution so that I wouldn't bring along a band of law-enforcement officers—they might learn that they were being hunted by the FBI. They probably had local law-enforcement contacts. If so, they might just disappear and take my Erin with them.

I couldn't take the chance. For now, my best bet was to stick with the same game plan, play ignorant of my knowledge that the compound appeared vacant, and hope they still wanted to trade the drugs for the girls.

I made it back to the highway, drove five miles west, did a U-turn and parked off the road about twenty feet. The risk, of course, was that a cop would see the car, stop, and offer help. Or realize the car was operating just fine and begin asking questions.

I turned on the phone and dialed the number. Carter answered, which brought some immediate relief that he hadn't gone dark on me.

He spoke in his typical blunt tone. "You are late."

"Can't help it. The Chrysler broke down."

I heard some angry words in another language.

"What is wrong with the car?" he asked.

"It just went dead, and I steered the car over to the side of the road. Battery, alternator…I don't know. And I don't know how to fix it." I paused an extra beat. "I guess I can walk the rest of the way. I think your lovely facility is only a few miles away. Might take me an hour, I'm guessing."

"But then you would leave the boxes alone? You're not very smart for an FBI agent, Alex Troutt."

He'd taken the first steps down my desired path—*I wasn't*

very smart. Progress.

He asked, "You do have the boxes still in your possession?"

"Why would I get rid of the one thing that will give me Erin and Becca? Of course I have the boxes."

"Ah, so you have been paying attention to the seriousness of this situation. You are actually quite astute."

Did he really just say that? What a prick. Condescending and then patronizing in mere seconds.

"So, what's the plan, Carter?"

I heard muffled voices—in English this time, which made me think he was speaking to Nixon. But for all I knew he had a gaggle of former presidents working for him.

"Okay," he said. "We will come to you."

Come to me. Did that mean he was bringing the girls? Or would they just try to fix the car? That option made me nervous. I might have to open the hood and start yanking on wires and hoses. Maybe they'd simply grab me and the boxes and then take me to their new complex. Or would they take the boxes and leave me? Or take me and kill me once we got to the new digs?

The permutations were almost endless. And none, from what I could see, led directly to a positive outcome. I had to let them know I wasn't just an absentminded follower. I did this for a single purpose.

"Are you bringing Erin and Becca with you?"

"We will come to you."

He sounded like one of those prerecorded telemarketers. Annoying as hell.

I gave him the exact location, although I was sure he could find me on their GPS tracker.

"How long until you get here? I don't want a highway patrolman showing up, searching the car, and then finding your two boxes."

I heard what sounded like a growl. "We'll be there in fifteen minutes."

He hung up the line. So, they were relatively close, maybe the same county. Might make sense, if he'd bribed local law-enforcement officials to turn a blind eye.

Would Carter bring the girls? He sounded noncommittal when I'd asked him, which made me think not.

I tapped my chin, pondering another question: should I open the hood and start ripping out hoses and cords, essentially making the car unfixable, at least not quickly? That would force them to take the boxes—and hopefully me—with them. But what if, for some reason, I needed to use the car?

Too many damn ways this could go. And something told me it wouldn't be without someone getting hurt. A couple of former presidents were at the top of my list to get their asses kicked.

Seventeen

Alex

A pair of headlights hit my eyes through the rearview. Sitting taller in the driver's seat, I wondered if this was Carter and Nixon. I tried to channel my connection with Erin to attempt to determine if she might also be in the approaching car. It sounded silly, unless you had kids of your own. Something about that bond was difficult to describe, yet unmistakable in its strength of signal.

I could feel my nerves jangling. My mouth became parched, and perspiration gathered at my hairline. I was anxious about how this might play out, but the most prominent feeling was almost a desperate longing to embrace Erin, to look into her eyes, to know that she was safe.

Oh, I wished that were so. But I couldn't fool myself. I'd never been one to swim in a sea of denial. And everything about this situation made it the most real, gut-wrenching experience of my life.

The car slowed down as it got closer. It was a black SUV. This had to be Carter and Nixon. It made a wide U-turn in front of my car—I'd decided to leave the hood up but not mess with any cables or hoses. The last thing I needed was to do something stupid that might injure me and negate my ability to rescue the girls.

It was a late-model Cadillac Escalade. The windows were almost as dark as the paint color. I hadn't seen this vehicle at the compound when I'd left yesterday. Maybe they had it hidden somewhere else on the property...a getaway car.

The SUV pulled to a stop just a few feet in front of the Chrysler. It had an imposing if not intimidating presence. Had they jacked it up an extra foot or so? Because of the bright lights shining in my face, I could only see the outline of the driver. He looked tall. The front passenger seat was empty.

Were Erin and Becca in the back seat?

I reached between my legs and felt the lump under the floorboard rug. The gun was out of sight, but easily retrievable if I needed to use it.

The door to the SUV opened, and the driver stepped out. For some reason, I felt compelled to do the same.

The man said, "Stop where you are."

It was Nixon.

I felt my heart thump my chest. I wasn't sure why I was having that reaction. I'd been almost certain he would be in the car. Maybe it was the setting—his cartoonish face illuminated by the glow of the headlights and brightening sky.

I didn't move as I watched him go to the back of the SUV and pull something out. He walked to the front, and I saw jumper cables in his hands. He opened the hood to the Escalade, placed the red and black clamps onto his battery, and then took the opposite end and did the same on the Chrysler's battery.

"Try to start the car now," he said.

As I slipped into the front seat, I was thankful he hadn't first tried to start the Chrysler to diagnose the problem. Point for me, I suppose. I turned the ignition, and of course, it started right up.

He pulled off the cables, closed both hoods, and tossed the cables into the back of the Escalade.

I was standing outside the Chrysler again when he marched in his cowboy boots back to the SUV.

"Follow me," he said.

"Are Erin and Becca in there?"

He stopped just before the door shut. "Follow me." Then he closed the door and began backing up the Escalade.

I ran back to the Chrysler, threw the gear into drive, made a quick U-turn, and gunned it. Nixon hadn't waited on me. He was already a good hundred yards in front of me. In fact, the whole car-fixing process seemed rehearsed, as if he'd done this type of thing before. It seemed more like a timed pit-stop—as if he wanted to ensure no one saw him on the side of the road.

The Chrysler caught up, and we cruised along at about seventy miles per hour for almost ten minutes. Then the SUV pulled into the parking lot of an abandoned gas station. I followed Nixon as he pulled around back, where there were two bays with doors pulled shut.

Did he need to take a leak? I had no idea what was going on. I leaned over, lifted the rug, and touched the grip of the pistol. I needed to be ready for anything.

Without warning, one of the bay doors started opening just like my automatic garage door at home. Nixon or someone must have punched a button. He pulled the Escalade into the garage and killed the engine. He began to get out of the SUV, and I clicked the button to roll down my window. But the bay door started shutting.

What the hell was going on? I almost yelled out, but I held back. For a few seconds, I sat in my idling car, wondering if this was another part of their scheme. I jerked my head around to see if someone might be sneaking up on me. It was all clear. Just a lot of rocks, a few shredded tires lying in the weeds, and the gas station that I'd thought was abandoned.

"Fuck!" I banged an open palm off the steering wheel. My pulse was doing double time. *What to do, what to do, what to do.*

I grabbed the pistol, swung open my door.

Just then, the second bay door began to open. With one foot still in the car, I lowered my gun hand to my side. A smaller white SUV, a Chevy of some sort, pulled out. It had a dented fender and mud streaks down the side. The driver's side window rolled down. It was Nixon again. "Follow me," he said.

"Where are Erin and Becca?"

"Follow me."

"Fuck that. Tell me where the girls are."

He looked straight ahead for a second. I had no idea what he was thinking. I couldn't see anyone else in the car—the vehicle didn't have tinted windows.

Then it hit me. Had he left the girls tied up in the back of the Escalade? And now he was trying to lure me away to another location where he and possibly Carter or others would take the drugs from me?

But what would that gain them—leaving the girls here?

I wasn't thinking clearly.

Nixon turned and stabbed a finger at the Chrysler. "Just follow me, and everything will work out. If you don't, bad things will happen to the girls."

He rolled up the window as I opened my mouth. He started to pull away.

Decision time. Follow Nixon and hope that he's telling the truth, or figure out a way inside this gas station to look for the girls, either in the car or maybe another part of the building. For a moment, I considered trying to do both—make a quick run into the building, if I could easily determine how to get inside, and hope like hell I'd find the girls but no one else.

The Chevy disappeared around the corner. I marched four steps toward the building.

A zap of doubt pinged my brain—I stopped in my tracks. Would Nixon actually leave the girls here, knowing I could walk in and find them before I handed over the drugs?

"Crap!" I raced back, jumped into the driver's seat, and threw the gearshift into drive. The Chrysler sprayed dust as I tore around the corner. The white Chevy was already on the highway headed west, the same direction we had been moving earlier.

In making the turn onto the highway, I didn't bother tapping the brakes. The Chrysler bobbed up and down like a small boat plowing through choppy waters, but it eventually gripped the concrete and started to catch up to the Chevy.

I saw a couple of cars moving in my direction. One of the two didn't bother with headlights. The skies were beginning to brighten. The lonely road would soon fill with more cars. I better understood Nixon's urgency—he didn't want to be seen jump-starting my car. And even after that, I now believed he'd changed vehicles simply to ensure no one would be able to trace him to the Escalade when he'd jump-started the car on the side of the road.

It was apparent this whole operation hadn't been devised just in the last week. Carter, Nixon...they might be scum-sucking slime, but they'd utilized some systematic processes to respond to every scenario thus far.

After another five minutes on the highway, just as we began climbing a small hill on a bend in the road, Nixon hit the brakes so hard I saw the Chevy's back end lurch forward. I wasn't close enough to hit him, but I dropped my speed in half in about a hundred feet. He swerved off the road and hooked a right. I followed him as the road turned to dirt and small rocks, although every few seconds, the Chrysler would lift up, thanks to a larger boulder embedded in the surface. I questioned how far off the highway Nixon was taking me. Was it to their backup compound? Maybe their sex-prison operation was at a totally different location, being run by other presidential bottom-feeders.

For a quick second, my mind could hear my dear friend, Ozzie, cracking jokes about presidents—politicians, in general—and various forms of parasites. Damn, I could have used his help on this one.

As I trailed Nixon over two ridges, I felt more alone than ever. The only advantage I had right now was the gun on the floorboard. But I knew if I ended up using it, the drugs-for-the-girls swap wouldn't have gone well.

We traveled through a dry creek bed and then down a hill. That's when I spotted a blue trailer on the floor of the canyon. My eyes didn't blink as we drove up to it. I parked about ten feet to the side of the Chevy. Nixon got out—he was still wearing his mask—and he waved me on as he walked toward the trailer's door. I clenched my jaw, which still hurt like hell, as I debated whether to trust Nixon.

I chose not to trust him.

I grabbed the gun and tucked it into the back of my khakis, pulling my shirt over it. "Are the girls in the trailer?" I asked.

He did another circle-wave. This guy wasn't big on talking.

"Nixon," I yelled.

He stopped at the bottom of the steps and flipped his head around. The mask bobbled like a blow-up doll. Again, no response. If nothing else, those frickin' masks would give me nightmares until my last days on earth, I was sure.

I was tempted to pull the gun right there and then. I could run up and put the gun at the base of Nixon's brain and officially call this a hostile trade. It might work.

Might.

I glanced at the two windows. They were covered, but that didn't mean a gun wasn't aimed right at my head. I might not even get the chance to run up to Nixon. And then what would happen to Erin and Becca?

Again, I erred on the side of caution. I caught up with Nixon as he pulled out a set of keys from his pocket.

"The girls are inside, right?" I'd lowered my volume.

"Yep," he said, focusing on finding the right key for the door.

If he was using a key, did that mean there was no one inside—not Carter or any other associated thug? Maybe Carter was off kidnapping more girls, whom he'd use as bait to force someone to do his dirty work. If so, that could mean that I had the advantage after all.

Adrenaline pumped my blood a little faster—if that were possible—as I placed my foot on the first step. It was made of wood, and it creaked when I put my full weight on it. As he fumbled with the keys, I did a quick three-sixty. Just a lot of rocks and dirt. Maybe this was the place from where all those conspiracy theorists had believed the wheeled robots had collected evidence to show there was water on Mars.

Lack of food and hydration was clearly getting to me.

"This one should work," Nixon finally said.

He turned the key and pulled the door open, bumping into me, causing me to take a step back. He walked inside the darkened space.

I suddenly had a déjà vu moment. *Crappy trailer with no lights* meant people were waiting to jump me once I was inside.

"You coming inside or not?" he said.

"I, uh…" I hesitated.

"Gotta find a light for this place." He disappeared inside the trailer.

My gut told me this wasn't right. But what was the alternative at this point—get in the Chrysler and drive back to the highway? I had no leverage.

I willed myself up the last two steps and poked my head inside. "Erin, Becca, are you in there?"

Nothing for a couple of seconds.

"They're in the back with me," Nixon said. "I had to put tape over their mouths because they wouldn't stop shouting."

I stepped all the way inside. I could barely see a hand in front of my face.

"I'm back here. Walk toward my voice," Nixon said.

Sounded like he was behind another door.

"Why aren't the lights turning on?"

"This piece-of-shit trailer has been empty for years."

With the door open, my eyes began adjusting to the darkness. Now my range was all of about five feet. I stumbled over a bump in the carpet but placed my hand against the wall to stay upright.

"Nixon, where are you?" I could barely make out a kitchen counter on the right-hand side. I kept shuffling forward.

Then I heard a car start.

The Chrysler. What the hell…?

I flipped around on my heels and backtracked out of the trailer. Just as I reached the door, I saw Carter behind the wheel, reversing the Chrysler. A thin wire jerked my neck backward.

"You little bitch!"

I was being strangled by Nixon. Gagging, I struggled to get my fingers under the wire.

"You thought you could stop us. Now you're going to die in the middle of nowhere." Nixon chuckled. "Vultures will get a nice snack. They're always looking for something a little meatier than a dead snake."

I could feel my head go red, and my eyes bulge—and I could

still see Carter driving off in the Chrysler. That had been their play all along. Use the carrot to bring me out here, then take off with the drugs while Nixon killed me.

I could feel the wire cutting into my skin. The smell of blood invaded my nostrils. I tried plucking at the wire, but I couldn't get a grip. I had to be the most naïve agent the FBI had ever produced. I'd been duped for the second time using the same darkened-trailer method.

But I quickly realized this time was different. Yes, Nixon's laughter filled my ear, and the sound of it made me sick to my stomach. This time, though, the door was open. I hooked my foot around the doorframe. At the same time, my right hand finally grabbed the wire. I pulled myself forward just a tad, then rammed my head backward with everything I had, cracking Nixon's nose. I could feel cartilage crunch like a bag of walnuts. He screamed, loosened his grip.

Blood went everywhere as I stumbled down the stairs and fell to the ground. I took in a precious breath and reached for my neck—I could feel the burn from where the wire had broken skin.

"You fucking bitch!" he roared.

I looked up to see the Chrysler disappearing around the rocky bend. But I also saw my gun. It had fallen out of my pants. I quickly looked over my shoulder. Nixon had ripped off his mask. His face was a bloody mess, his expression was full of rage. He barreled down the stairs, his eyes on the gun. I got to my knees and tried to push up to standing.

A heavy boot landed on my back, and I face-planted in the dirt. Nixon had used me as a launching pad. He was laughing and grunting at the same time. I jumped from the ground and raced for the gun. But he had a head start on me.

He scooped up the gun. But as he twisted around, I reached down, grabbing a handful of dirt. As soon as he faced me, I chucked the dirt at his eyes.

The gun fired over my shoulder, and I flinched. But he stumbled back, yelling because of the dirt in his eyes. He let the gun drop to his side. I had a chance.

I ran forward and swung my leg upward between his legs. He turned at the last second—my foot missed its target and bounced off his thigh.

Dammit!

Just as he brought the gun up again, I hit him with a roundhouse punch in the nose. This time, he squealed like a piggy. The gun went flying over his shoulder. I ran past him, but he tripped me up. I tasted dirt again. I looked up, couldn't find the gun. My eyes darted left and right—it was as though the weapon had been camouflaged in burnt orange, the color of the dirt. I frantically crawled around, sifting my hands across the dirt, hoping I'd feel the gun. I could hear myself begin to cry out loud. It was like I was having an out-of-body experience. But I knew if I didn't get to that gun, Erin and Luke wouldn't have a mother.

Was Erin even alive?

I pushed the thought away as I scrambled farther away from Nixon, searching for the gun.

Where's the fucking gun?

The absence of Nixon's rage snagged my attention. Where was Nixon? I looked over my shoulder—he was running for the Chevy.

That fucker couldn't get away, not if he knew where Erin was.

By some miracle, I finally spotted the gun. I snagged it and took off in the direction of the Chevy. The vehicle was spinning its wheels, moving in reverse. Dirt and pebbles hit me like I was caught in a Texas tornado. I lifted an arm to block my eyes, but I still brought the gun up and fired a shot. It hit metal.

I quickly shifted to my right to move out of the way of the sandstorm until I faced the front of the Chevy. Nixon was still going in reverse. I lifted the gun and ran toward the vehicle. I didn't know where he was going—the rocky road back to the highway was on the other side of me—but he was moving at a faster clip. I stopped, brought up my other hand to steady my aim, and fired three quick rounds.

The vehicle jerked hard to the right, then crashed into a boulder twice its size. Aside from the spray of dust lingering in the air, everything went still. I looked through the haze. Was that Nixon's head resting against the steering wheel? With my gun still raised, I walked to the vehicle—I veered to the passenger side so I could see if he was pretending to be knocked out while holding some weapon out of my line of sight.

Peering through the window, I saw his head lying against the steering wheel. No sign of a deployed airbag. The car was probably too old to have one. His hands hung to the floorboard like dead limbs from a tree. His hair was matted to his face, with a fair amount of blood. I couldn't see his eyes.

I wasn't even sure he was breathing. Part of me wanted him dead, but that wouldn't help Erin and Becca. He had to be lucid so I could quiz him on the location of the girls. I opened the door, put a foot into the cabin.

He roared, swung his arm, and connected with my jaw. I was stunned and dropped to the seat. He growled again, threw the gear into drive, and punched the gas. I flew backward, almost falling out of the speeding car. He flipped the wheel left and right, trying to throw me out. I grabbed the swinging door and pulled myself up. In the process, I'd let go of the gun. His eyes saw it at the same time mine did.

I thrust myself into the cabin and lunged for the gun. I got to it just after his hand took hold of it. He still had one hand on the steering wheel, but he wasn't watching where we were going. I didn't know what else to do, so I bit down on his wrist until I tasted blood.

He cried out, and the SUV swung wildly. He let go of the steering wheel and yanked on my hair. He finally jerked his sweaty wrist out from my teeth, fumbling with the gun. We were still moving. I threw my body at him, pawing at the gun while throwing punches at his face and his body. He screamed, cursing at me. I kept going, but so did he.

He finally got a good hold of the gun and aimed it at me. I grabbed his wrist with both hands and shoved it away—and then we crashed. I heard the gun fire just as my body slammed into the dashboard.

I moaned and lifted my eyes. That was when I saw a man with no face—he'd shot himself in the face when we crashed into the trailer. I closed my eyes, crawled out of the SUV, and dropped to the dirt. I was alive, but the man who knew where my daughter was had just died.

I wanted to die, too.

Eighteen

Ivy

Over the course of a couple of minutes, I rang the doorbell three times. I struck out each time. I stepped back and took note of the Mazda sedan in the driveway. I wasn't certain, but I believed that car belonged to Jill Bailey.

The skies were overcast, which matched my mood at the moment. Checking up on a mother who might be neglecting her child sent a plethora of memories flashing to the front of my mind. During my tenure as a special investigator for CPS, I'd witnessed some of the most horrific conditions for any human being to be living in, let alone a child. I'd also heard countless excuses and justifications. Lies.

I wasn't oblivious to the struggles parents experienced—stress, these days, could hit at any time from almost any direction, including job, lack of money, relationships, mental-health issues, social media, you name it. But none of that rationalized neglecting, abusing, or murdering a child. The tough part, though, came after pulling the child from the home and placing them with foster parents. Far too often, the foster parents would abuse the kids. It was a cycle that seemed almost impossible to break inside a system that the government refused to fix.

I forced out a breath like I was pushing smoke into the air. I could feel my stomach lock into a big knot, knowing the memories of my foster experiences sat on the other side of the floodgates. I'd been given up for adoption at birth. At one point a couple of years back, I tried to locate my parents. I thought we'd made some progress, but an investigator who supposedly had some knowledge to share with me had died in a traffic accident. That was when I realized it just wasn't meant to be. I looked to the future instead and learned to treasure my friendships, including the one that had lit a fire in me: Saul.

"I'll be there in a minute!"

A shout from inside the house. Finally. That had to be Jill. Good that she was home, but I also knew she could be playing the delay game if—I had to remind myself...*if*—she was as Gerald had described: a strung-out addict who was so desperate that she'd essentially paid off a drug debt with her own child.

Three deep breaths as I waited outside the front door.

I thought about the research I'd done last night after Saul had dozed off. I'd slipped out of bed and into the living room, and opened my laptop.

I read countless opioid-addiction stories, how it was the biggest health crisis in the country. I learned there were many forms of opioids—some natural, some synthetic. Their original purpose was for pain relief. But it was their addictive qualities—physically and psychologically—that had pushed the drugs into a stratosphere that had destroyed thousands of lives and families. Fentanyl, which was created by a scientist at a pharmaceutical company way back in 1960, was fifty times more potent than heroin. Pills that dissolved in the cheeks were the most popular form of the drug, although variations included patches, lollipops, and tongue films.

I also saw a number of street terms that were used for fentanyl, including China girl, tango and cash, king ivory, and murder eight, among others.

I could hear the click of a deadbolt unlatching, and then the door opened about a foot.

"Yes, can I help you?" A woman's eyes looked clownish. At first, I thought it might have been a joke—had she purposely applied enough makeup to where she'd glow in the dark? But then another thought hit me. She could be covering up her usual gaunt look.

"Hi, I'm Ivy Nash, and I wanted to see if you had a few minutes to talk."

"About what? And who did you say you were with?" Her voice had this singsong timbre to it, as if she were a receptionist at a car dealership. Fake.

"I worked for CPS for five years."

"CPS." She went monotone as she swung open the door.

I didn't think she'd caught my use of the past tense: *worked*. I wasn't going to explain it to her. And it also told me that the real CPS had yet to show up. Disappointing, yes. Surprising, no.

I saw the open door as an invitation to walk in—my old CPS responses were almost instinctive. Once inside, my mouth formed an O. The clownish makeup face was still there, but so was the rest of the woman. What was left of her. She wore a pair of blue sweats that hung off her as if she were seven years old and wearing her mother's clothes. Her long-sleeve T-shirt was stained in several places. I could see the bones popping out on her shoulders and at the elbows.

"You want to talk to me?" she asked, her tone suddenly defensive.

A quick glance around the living area. Toys were everywhere, but so was everything else. It looked like someone had ransacked the place. I picked up a waft of something foul, and my nose twitched.

"Is something burning?"

"Oh shit. Lila!" she shouted. She slammed the front door and shuffled toward the kitchen. If she was overly concerned, her speed wasn't showing it. The bottoms of her sweats dragged on the floor. I spotted a three-inch piece of fabric that had torn at the end and was hanging by just a few threads. I wondered if that was symbolic of her life.

As she disappeared into the kitchen, I inched my way inside a little farther and stopped, waited.

"What the fuck, Lila...?" she shouted from the other room.

My body went tight.

"The toaster wasn't working right, so I pushed the button again," Lila said apologetically.

"I told you, dammit, you only push it once, that's it. Fuck! If you can't do anything right, then just wait for me. Do you hear me?"

It felt like a metal pole had been fused to my spine. I almost said something, but I held back—for now.

"Yes, Mom." The girl sounded dejected. Who wouldn't be, especially at the age of seven?

Seven years old.

I heard what sounded like a metal utensil clanging into a sink.

"There. Eat," Jill said.

Jill shuffled around the corner, her pace no different than before. Normally, a guest of the house might look away or have a magazine in hand, pretending to look through it. I did neither. I calmly looked her in the eye. Gerald had asked—no, pleaded—for me to visit with Jill and make my own assessment. In some respects, he was my client, although nothing formal had been signed.

"Are you having a tough morning, Jill?"

She crossed her arms under her chest, leaned into her hip—it was like looking at a clothed skeleton. "Why would you ask that?"

"Because of the way you were speaking to your daughter."

The muscles in her jaw twitched. She was pissed, upset, maybe both.

"Can you give me a minute?" She held up a finger and walked down a hallway without allowing me time to respond.

The description Gerald had given of his wife, up to now, had been spot-on. I waited about twenty seconds. "Jill," I called out.

No response.

"Jill, I have four other appointments I need to make before noon, so can you please come out here?"

I started counting. One, two, three, four... Then, I started down the hallway. She popped out of a room and shut the door behind her.

"I'm right here. Just had to use the restroom."

Her voice already sounded more relaxed. Had she taken one of those dissolving pills? She followed me into the living room as Lila came around the corner from the kitchen.

"Can I have some orange juice?" the little girl asked as she entered the living room. Her eyes met mine. She remembered me.

"Hi there." I crouched down to meet her at eye level.

"Hi," she said. "How's my daddy doing?"

I could feel Jill's eyes on me. Her head went back and forth between her daughter and me. "Do you two...? Wait." She put a finger to her chin, and then she looked straight into my eyes.

"Are you the woman who rescued my daughter from my maniac husband?"

I lifted to my feet, not exactly sure how I wanted to respond to her question. I kept it simple. "Yes."

She took me in her arms and hugged my neck. "God bless you," she said as if she'd lost half her lung capacity. "That man turned into the devil. He abused me. He abused Lila."

She began to sniffle, but she didn't let go of my neck. It started to hurt, so I gently attempted to pull her off. I could see this wasn't going to be easy.

Nineteen

Ivy

A tear slid from Jill's eye. "When he kidnapped Lila, I had no idea what he was going to do to her."

"Daddy's a good person, Mom. He's my daddy." Lila's green eyes welled with tears.

"You stay out of this, Lila," Jill said. "You were a victim in this, just like me. But this is an adult problem."

"I want to see Daddy."

"You're not going to be seeing him for a while." Jill glanced at me for a quick second. "Your daddy needs to learn a lesson for breaking the law."

"He said he was just trying to keep me safe from you."

Jill tried to laugh, but there was no humor behind it. "Don't be silly, Lila. Your mother loves you. I'm not perfect. And I tell you 'sorry' when I mess up, just like you tell me. We're a team, right?"

The girl ran her hand along the back of the sofa. "I just want to see my daddy." Her voice was more serious now. She looked at me. "Will you help me see my daddy, please?"

Jill's intensity spiked. "Lila, what did I say?"

I couldn't take any more. "Hey, Lila, why don't you show me

your room?"

"Is that really necessary?" Jill moved a foot to her left, which happened to block my direct path down the hallway. She thought I was CPS and she was *still* pushing the envelope.

"Yes, it is." I took Lila by the hand, and the child walked me into her room.

I'd seen messy rooms, but this one looked like a bomb had been detonated. Toys and clothes were scattered everywhere. The mattress had no sheets or blanket.

Jill pulled up behind me.

"I was just about to change her sheets," she said, wiping her eyes and causing her eyeliner to smudge down her cheek. She didn't seem to know…or care.

"Can you give us a couple of minutes?" I asked Jill.

"You want to be with my daughter in my house, alone?" She was jabbing her finger at the floor.

"Yes, I do."

She didn't know it, but I wasn't giving an option. If she'd said no, I was prepared to walk out of the house with the little girl.

"Okay. I guess that's okay."

She left, and I started playing with Lila. She seemed to be most interested in playing with a K'NEX building set. She put together a helicopter as I sat there and tried to connect a few pieces into what looked like a raft. I was no engineer, but Lila, I could see, appeared enthralled with the process. Maybe it was her great escape from the chaos around her. We all needed something.

I asked her a few questions, and she gave me brief responses. I could sense she didn't want her mom to get in trouble, but most kids can't help but be transparent. It wasn't until they were older and jaded that they learned the art of lying to achieve a greater goal.

Once I got the information I needed, she said she wasn't hungry and she wanted to stay in her room and play.

I found Jill sitting on the couch, wringing her hands. She stood up as soon as I walked in.

"So, did I pass the test?"

"I haven't searched the home, Jill, but if I did, would I find more fentanyl somewhere?"

She shook her head in disgust. "You've been listening to Gerald's lies. He thinks just because I've lost a couple of pounds and I'm a bit moody that I'm some whacked-out drug addict. He's nuts. And what he's doing is covering up his own abuses."

"When did he hurt you?"

"I don't know. Sometime last week, I guess."

"How?"

"He, uh, pushed me down. I hurt my back." Her eyes darted around like a bird's. Then she snapped her fingers. "That's why I'm taking pain pills." She began to rub her back. "Yep, doctor says I might need surgery. For now, though, he gave me a pain reliever. Does a pretty good job. Says I have to stay on top of it, though, or the pain will get the best of me."

"Can you give me your doctor's name?"

"Dr. Mike...no, Mark Patterson."

I followed her eyes to a bookshelf. On it, I saw a James Patterson book.

Addicts think they can outwit anyone. But when they're desperate, they're the opposite of smart. I found it both maddening and pathetic.

"Why were you fired from your job, Jill?"

"I quit."

"The hospital would confirm that?"

"They'd lie to you just like Gerald has, apparently." She

rubbed both hands against her face—the makeup now looked more like a surreal painting. "Everyone is taking advantage of me, Ivy. But I'm not going to give up. I know when I'm being victimized."

I was certain she truly believed she was the poster child for the cause.

"Jill, where is your other daughter?"

"Other daughter." She studied me for a second, then went back to the bookshelf as if it held all the answers.

"Angel." I had to remind her?

"I know who my daughter is. I just miss her like any mother would. That's normal."

That last part sounded like a question, as if she needed me to validate her feelings.

"Where is Angel, Jill?"

It was as though her body shriveled up even more. She shuffled back two steps. "She's at my sister's place in California."

"When's the last time you spoke to Angel?"

"I don't know. Within the last week, I think."

"How was she?"

Her eyes drifted off.

"Jill?"

"Sorry."

"How was your daughter when you last spoke to her?"

"Fine. Just doing teenage stuff."

"Is she going to school?"

She nodded. "She's a real beauty. My sister knows people, says she can help her get modeling gigs, and from there, maybe get her introduced to producers."

And how many stories had come out recently about girls being abused by certain Hollywood power brokers? Was this woman paying attention to the world around her? Then again, Gerald didn't believe Angel was at her sister's place.

"Do you talk to your sister often?"

"Oh yeah, we're pretty close. She's my main support system, especially with Gerald going off the rails. He's such a prick. You have no idea."

For a split second, she sounded pretty convincing. If we'd been talking over the phone, if her appearance hadn't been so jarring, or if I hadn't witnessed what I had over the last few minutes, I might have believed her. Still, though, I couldn't automatically think that Gerald was a saint. Maybe he was caught up in this mess as well. The blame game worked both ways, and from my experience, rarely did I see one person tell the complete truth. But right now, it wasn't about splitting hairs on owning the most mistakes in a relationship. Addiction created fissures that were a mile wide and a mile deep.

"Do you have a cell phone?" I asked.

She looked at me as though I'd grown a third eye. "Uh, yeah." She found it on the coffee table under some empty fast-food wrappers and held it up.

"Call her."

She pondered my blunt direction. A few seconds ticked off, but my gaze stayed right on her.

"She's busy. At work now."

"Call her, Jill. Your daughter's well-being is on the line."

"What do you mean? Angel's fine."

"Is she?"

I could see her chin begin to quiver. I wondered if she was crumbling on the inside.

"Did you give your daughter to a drug dealer to pay off your debt?"

The quiver became more pronounced. I gave her a couple of

seconds, but that was all.

"Jill, we can get you help. But I'm worried about Angel. Do you know where she is?"

She took in a breath, but when she exhaled, it came out in bursts of sobs. "Dear God..." Her whole body shook as if she'd been locked in a freezer.

"Jill, we can't waste any time if she's not with your sister. Gerald said a man came by your house, claiming he was owed five thousand dollars. He waved a gun, basically threatened Lila. That's why Gerald took Lila, isn't it?"

A shaky nod as tears streamed down her face, which looked like something out of a horror flick. It was bad when I'd first arrived, but now... *my God.*

"Did you give some man your daughter in return for paying off your drug debt?"

She just sat there now. The tears had stopped. Her eyes looked straight ahead, unblinking. She seemed catatonic. I was witnessing a mental breakdown.

"Jill, who took your daughter? What's his name?"

More silence.

I moved over and took hold of her shoulders. "Jill, are you listening to me? Angel could be in serious trouble right now. Who knows what this guy has her doing? You've got to tell me who took her."

She kept looking over my shoulder, but I could feel her shivering through my arms. I was on the verge of losing her. "Jill, please tell me."

"Mom?"

I looked over and saw Lila holding her helicopter.

"Where is Angel?" the little girl asked.

She must have overheard me. I stood up straight. "Lila, I think everything is going to be okay," I said. "Your mom is upset.

Can you give us a moment?"

Lila looked at her helicopter. "Angel used to help me build things with my K'NEX. I miss her."

"I know you do, sweetie. And we're going to bring her home." I hoped like hell I wasn't lying to the little girl.

"Do you know when?"

"Not right now. That's what we're trying to figure out. So, can you go build something that she might like?"

She bit her lower lip. "She always used to build these robotic animals. I'll make her a robotic dog."

"Great idea."

She walked back to her room, and I turned to her mother, whose gaze hadn't even moved to look at her youngest daughter. Was she at a point where she was unreachable? I wondered if I needed to call Stan and see if we might need to get her committed to an institution. But first, I needed a name.

I sat next to her on the couch and put my hand on hers. "Jill, I can see how painful this is for you. It's got to hurt. But it's not too late. We can help Angel. *You* can help Angel. Just please give me a name."

Nothing.

I looked ahead for a moment. I reached into my pocket and took out my phone. I saw a text from Cristina. Something about the meeting with the school district had been moved to another time today. I'd deal with that later. I scrolled through my recent calls until I found Stan's number.

"Bennie Baldwin," Jill said. "That's the fucker who took my daughter."

"How do you reach him?"

More silence.

"Jill, how do you reach this Bennie person?"

"I call a voicemail. Then he calls me back. Sometimes I meet him somewhere."

Baldwin had to be screening his calls. An extra form of security. "Where do you meet him?"

"It changes, but usually in Navarro Park."

I put a hand to the side of my head. *Navarro Park.* "Is that off Commerce in western San Antonio?"

Jill blinked, but she was back in her catatonic state.

"Jill, I need for you to call Baldwin and set up a time to get some more pills."

Her eyes shifted to me. "More pills?" She sounded like a little kid asking for more dessert.

"Jill, this is about Angel. You want to help your daughter, right?"

She nodded slowly.

"Then you need to set up a time to meet Baldwin. I'll go in your place and find out where Angel is."

"Okay," she said with a sigh. But she didn't act.

I lifted her hand that held the phone. "Are you going to call him, or do I need to dial the number?"

She swallowed and sighed again. It was as though I'd asked her to run a marathon. I was about to slap her back into reality. "Jill." I couldn't let my anger get the best of me. Lila might hear me and become upset. That was the last thing she needed.

"Okay, okay," Jill finally said. She tapped the phone a few times and then put the phone to her ear.

"Go ahead and tell him in the voicemail that you've got the money to pay off the debt."

"But I don't. And he'll hurt us unless I pay him off."

"I'll have the police put you and Lila in protective custody if necessary."

She left the voicemail. Her voice cracked half the time, but I was sure he was used to hearing calls like that.

"How long until he calls back?" I asked.

"A couple of minutes."

"Can I get you some water?" I walked toward the kitchen when I heard her phone buzzing in her hand. I quickly jogged back. She looked at me for a second. I nodded. "You can do this, Jill. For Angel."

She swallowed and punched up the call. "Hey, Bennie."

I leaned in closer to hear his voice.

"What do you know—someone gets desperate and they call the Ben-master." He chuckled. "You got my five grand?"

"Yep."

"How you'd do it?"

"You got your ways. I got mine."

"That's my Jilly. Crafty when you need to be. Right, Jilly?"

"Sure, Bennie. When can I get my pills?"

A slight pause.

"Same park. One hour. Don't forget the five grand on your debt, plus five hundred for today. You got that, Jilly?"

"I got it, Bennie."

"Good."

The line went dead.

Jill tossed the phone on the table, put both hands over her face, and began to sob. "I sold my daughter to a drug dealer. What kind of mother am I?"

"You need to get help, Jill. You need to go to a detox center and not come out until you're clean and you can take care of Lila."

She nodded. "You're right. But what about Lila?"

"You need to tell the police that Gerald didn't do anything wrong."

"But he…" She put a fist over her mouth, then shook her head as if she were trying to rid herself of all the hate and vitriol.

"There's always a 'but' with me, isn't there?"

She was seeing the light, at least temporarily. Yet I knew her clairvoyance might last no more than an hour or two. Even addicts with the best intentions could be robbed of their thoughts by the smallest things. These were called "triggers," because they opened the door to the side of the brain that included fear and control. Combining those two emotions in the wrong way, for some, created a mix so toxic that it sent them spiraling…mentally, emotionally, and even physically.

The strange thing was that those triggers could come from something as mundane as the smell of a certain kind of food or a certain phrase used by somebody they don't even know. It would remind them of a time when they had suffered trauma. And in mere minutes, a positive person could be a very desperate person, willing to do anything to get their fix. Apparently, that included selling your daughter, in Jill's case.

"I don't want to give you excuses, Jill. It's important you own your decisions. But you're starting in the right direction." I saw a framed picture on a side table of girl with a headful of curls and a wide smile. I picked it up. "Is this Angel?"

Jill nodded, fighting back tears.

"Mind if I take a quick picture of it?"

She shrugged indifference, so I took the picture out of the frame and took a picture using my phone. I dialed Stan's number while glancing out the front window. I saw a woman getting out of her car. She had a portfolio tucked under her arm. She didn't look familiar, but I was almost certain she was with CPS. I told Jill that I needed to speak with someone out front, and then I stepped outside and asked the woman to hold up a minute before going inside.

Stan had just answered the phone. I explained the situation to both of them, starting with Jill admitting that Gerald was not at fault and that she would go into a detox center. I said it was important that Gerald—and not a foster parent—take care of Lila. Stan said he only needed a statement from Jill to start the process of releasing Gerald. I asked the CPS caseworker if she would wait with Jill and Lila until Stan sent an officer over. The woman said she would, and then she went inside. I walked to my car, still on the line with Stan.

"Didn't you say something about another daughter?" he asked.

"I did, yes."

"And what's the scoop?"

I knew if I brought up what I was about to do, Stan would throw a shit fit. He'd demand that he and the police get involved. But I knew we didn't have time for that. I also knew that if Bennie saw any cops around, he might disappear into the bowels of San Antonio. If that occurred, we might never find Angel. And this was still under the assumption that she was still alive. I hadn't wanted to upset Jill any further, but I had doubts about Angel's safety at this point. She'd been away from her home for over a week, and she hadn't reached out to her parents. If that were true, then, most likely, she wasn't in control of her own actions. She was either being held against her will, so drugged out that she didn't know which way was up, or she'd been killed.

I decided to tell Stan a partial truth. "Jill says her teenage daughter, Angel, is staying with her sister in California."

"Do you believe her?"

"Do you believe anything an addict says?" I countered.

"Point for you."

We agreed to keep in touch. I got in Black Beauty, called up Cristina, and explained the plan that I'd just thought of.

Twenty

Alex

A wet goo coated my skin. I knew it had to be part of the brain matter and other parts of Nixon's face. My only remorse was not getting information on the whereabouts of Erin and Becca. Now, I had nothing. I had less than nothing. My mind spiraled into a hopeless abyss.

I lay on the ground for a period of time, literally eating dirt—it crunched between my teeth. My muscles felt like they'd been zapped of all their power. The sun hit me like a laser on the side of my face, and my neck stung from the wire Nixon had used to strangle me. My jaw was still sore from when I'd been punched. And none of it mattered. I'd let down Erin and Becca, and now I might never see my daughter again.

The gears in my battered mind cranked just enough to try to understand Carter's endgame. He knew that if I survived the perverted advances of Grant Valdez, I would have ended up back at the compound. I would have called him and asked where everyone was. The fact that I pretended the car had broken down before I reached the compound could have made their lack of an explanation that much easier.

Instead, Nixon swapped out cars at the abandoned gas station and insisted I follow him out here. Maybe they thought I had contacted law enforcement, after all, and so they were taking precautions to protect their sex prison and their drug-trafficking business. They'd actually moved their entire lurid operation—at least it seemed so—because they thought I might bring the heat with me. But to be sure all was safe, they'd lured me into this desolate canyon to make sure I wasn't being followed.

I pondered the possible street value of the drugs in the back of the Chrysler. Had to be seven figures, if not eight.

The drugs and Carter were gone, though. And my daughter wasn't in the trailer. Part of me knew something was up when Nixon had waved at me to follow him. I'd wanted to find her so badly that I let irrational thoughts drive my actions. Not that anything I could have done would make Erin appear out of thin air. But I could have put the gun on Nixon and threatened him until he told me the truth. Of course, Carter had been hiding nearby, so it was anyone's guess exactly how it would have played out.

Erin. My sweet little girl. My independent, brave daughter.

Back to the endgame. Where was she? What had Carter done with her and Becca? Were they at the new compound, and where was that? Had they been taken to Carter's personal residence? Could he have just discarded them on the side of the road? That was wishful thinking. And then the opposite thought stabbed at my heart: were they even alive?

I squeezed my eyes so hard I felt something akin to a brain freeze. Tears rolled off my face. A few found my open neck wound—reminding me that *I* was alive. Reminding me that I'd failed to find Erin, to protect Erin. A mother should never outlive her children. The circle of life wasn't meant to work that way.

"Oh God, why?" I clawed at the ground until I felt the pressure of dirt under my fingernails. "Why, why, whyyyy?" My voice bounced off the rocky walls.

And then I thought I heard something else.

I stopped moving. I stopped breathing. Maybe it was a hallucination.

"Mom!"

An echo. I shot up to a sitting position and looked all around me. Nothing. My mind was playing games. Tears welled in my eyes again.

"Mom, it's me!"

It was like a burst of a supernova—I saw Erin running out from behind the trailer. Becca was right behind her. I jumped to my feet, rubbed my eyes again, still not completely convinced of what I was seeing.

"Erin?" I couldn't catch my breath. "Erin!"

She barreled into me, and we hugged like we'd never hugged before. Becca came up, and I put an arm around her, and the three of us didn't let go…couldn't let go.

"Erin, where were you?"

She pulled back, and I saw the deep scrape down her cheek. I reached for her face, but she turned her cheek away.

"Are you okay, Erin? What did they do to you…to both of you?"

Erin and Becca glanced at each other. The kind of glance that said there were things they didn't want to repeat. Tears formed in Becca's eyes.

"You don't have to tell me, Becca."

She took in a breath. Her cheeks were pink, which accentuated all the freckles on her face. Both girls looked like they'd been dragged through a mud pit.

"Honestly," she said, gasping out a breath, "I'm not completely sure."

"They smacked us around some," Erin interjected. "So don't

freak out when you see some bruises on my back and stomach."

I took Erin's head in my hands and studied her cut. She pushed my hands away. "Mom, I'm okay." Her eyes went to Becca. I followed her gaze.

"Becca, do you want to share anything?"

"Well, after they put that needle in my arm—later…I don't know exactly when—I remember waking up, and…" She looked at Erin, and then they grabbed hold of each other's hand. Becca continued with her head down. "I didn't have on any clothes, and some man was getting out of bed. He had long hair tied back in a ponytail. He was real skinny. I think he was on something. Well, just about everyone we met was on something. But I think he did stuff to me." She put a hand to her head as tears poured from her eyes.

Erin took her in her arms. I wrapped my arms around both girls. "I'm so sorry, Becca. We will find the people who did this, and they will be punished. You have my promise on that."

She sniffled. "Thanks. I'm just not sure that will take away the nightmares," she said, her voice barely audible. Then, with her glistening eyes, she looked at her best friend. "But with friends like Erin, I have hope. She was so strong throughout this whole thing."

I took a long look at my daughter. She knew I was looking at her, but she focused on Becca. Erin wasn't breaking down or losing it. How was this possible?

"Erin, are you okay…I mean, besides your face?"

"We saw them murder a girl." Erin's lower lip quivered.

"Oh no…" I shook my head. "When? How?"

She huffed out a breath, pushed hair out of her face, as if that would give her the fortitude to continue. "Right after we escaped. It was when they were moving everyone. I found a baseball bat, and I hit this one guy on the head with it. We ran off, tried to get some other girls to go with us. But they were either too scared or too drugged up to move."

"Where did you go?"

"At first, we just ran, and then we stopped once we got behind this hill with rocks. We looked back and wondered if we could figure out a way to rescue some of the other girls."

I shook my head, my jaw hanging open. "So when did you see this other girl, you know…?"

"Just after that. I remembered her from inside. At one point, she told me she was from Texas, but that's all I got out of her. When we were all ushered out of the building, she was so whacked out, she could hardly move. They started smacking her around outside. And then, out of nowhere, the guy who wore the Jimmy Carter mask came up with a pistol and shot her in the head."

I almost choked on a piece of dirt.

"Yeah, Ms. T., they buried her behind the shed," Becca added. "We watched them dig a hole and dump her body in there." She took in a ragged breath.

I looked at Erin. She nodded. "It's something I'll never forget. That poor girl. But all of them are being abused, Mom. It's so sad, and I just don't know how it can go on and no one knows about it. There were men in and out of that place all the time."

"Nothing happened to you?" I asked.

"Like I said, they beat us up. But I fought back pretty hard. Kicked this one guy in the nuts, and then I grabbed his needle and broke it."

The girls giggled. I tried. "But did you end up…?"

"They never put their China town or tango and cash, or whatever you want to call that crap…they never gave it to me. Well, they tried to get me to swallow a pill, but I spit it out. I felt a little woozy after that, but I still stayed awake."

I wondered what they were planning for Erin since she hadn't let them drug her and force her to have sex with their so-called customers.

She put a hand to her cheek. "After I kicked the guy in the nuts, he got mad. He had one guy hold me down, and he took a razor blade and cut me. I screamed bloody murder."

I touched my own cheek and imagined the pain that Erin had endured. It felt like someone had taken pruning shears to my heart.

"Yeah, I think I might have heard her screaming. It scared me," Becca said.

The girls grabbed hands again. Damn, I was glad they had each other during this ordeal.

"Erin, you're still the most beautiful girl I've ever seen."

"Mom." She had mastered saying my name using two syllables.

I looked at Becca. "You're beautiful too, Becca. And both of you are so brave." I glanced around. "But how did you two end up here?"

"Just dumb luck," Erin said. "We knew we couldn't get near the road, so we just kept walking deeper into the hills. We were hoping to find another house, but we were so far off the road, we wondered if we might just get lost and never be found. We were on the other side of that hill when we heard cars driving. When we got to the top and looked down, we saw you and that guy in the Nixon mask fighting. Well, at first, we didn't know it was you. But after a minute, I told Becca I was pretty sure it was you." Her eyes went to the SUV where Nixon's body was. I saw flies hovering around the window.

"Mrs. T., you were badass. You killed that guy, didn't you?" Becca had a smile on her face.

"Kind of. The gun just went off when we were struggling, and the SUV hit the trailer. Anyway, we need to get out of here and get you back to your parents at the hotel. From there, we can clean up, get law enforcement involved, and try to find these—"

"They're nothing but a bunch of cowardly fuckers, Mrs. T. I say we castrate all of them."

I couldn't argue with any of that. We started the long trek back into the city.

Twenty-One

Ivy

Dark clouds had rolled in, and I wondered if it might rain. I stood in a bed of mulch near a vacant swing set in Navarro Park. The space was surrounded by evergreens. It felt very secluded for being in the city. I was alone, other than Cristina, who was perched in a live oak about thirty yards away.

"You see anything?" I had an open phone line to her and had tucked my phone in my front shirt pocket.

"A few people walking down the sidewalk," she said. "I hope this guy shows up soon. Sitting in a tree is fucking brutal on my ass."

Cristina. Just as crass as always.

"Once you see anyone heading into the park, put your phone on mute."

"Roger, that," she said.

I watched a flock of birds in a V formation fly overhead. It appeared they were trying to escape the pending bad weather. Maybe there was some symbolism there, since I was, once again, forging right ahead into what could be perceived as a dangerous situation.

"*Perceived*," I said out loud, mocking my own justification for acting as though I were about to meet with a real-estate agent.

I wasn't fond of parks—I'd once been kidnapped from one,

and then later tortured. But in the daylight, I had less anxiety. And just knowing Cristina was close by gave me comfort. She had a specific purpose in my grand plan, but if something went awry, she could call Stan.

Stan. Yep. I could see his face turning red once I told him what I'd done. But he should know that I wasn't going to wait until he got approval from umpteen layers of government bureaucracy before putting together what they would call a sting operation. I just called it a method to figure out where Angel Bailey was. After that, I'd likely get Stan and his team to raid whatever location Baldwin had her stashed.

If she was still alive. I hoped.

"Quick walker headed your way. Carrying some type of grocery bag," Cristina said.

I casually turned and saw a man with a thin beard walking into the park. He slowed down, turning his head from side to side. He had to be looking for Jill.

Without preamble, I walked out of the mulch over to the bench and sat down. I crossed my legs and began moving one up and down, my arms crossed. Anxiety was the vibe I was shooting for. It only took about thirty seconds before he approached me.

"Hey, have you see another woman around here?"

I peered up and saw the man I believed to be Baldwin, wearing jeans so baggy I wondered if he had an ass. He was slight of build, and I immediately thought he wasn't just a dealer—he was also a user.

"Nope," I said, still kicking my leg as if it were being controlled by some unknown force.

He glanced around the park again and then dropped his eyes back to me. I shimmied my shoulders—as if I were freezing. It was probably eighty degrees even under cloudy skies.

He pulled out a pack of cigarettes, smacked one end against

the palm of his hand, then slipped out a stick and lit it. He took his first drag, and smoke streamed out the side of his mouth. I'd heard it takes ten thousand hours to become an expert at anything. I felt certain this man was a master at smoking cigarettes.

"You look like you could use a fix." He cracked a smile across his weathered face, then blew more smoke out the other side of his mouth. A gust of wind sent it back my way. I also picked up a waft of something akin to tacos and BO. I tried not to retch.

"It depends."

"Depends?" He laughed mockingly. "I know a junkie when I see one."

Or maybe a good actress. "Are you Bennie?"

He stopped moving with his cigarette an inch from his mouth. "How do you know my name?"

He'd just answered my question. A second later, I got the first visual of what Cristina was tasked with doing. He would soon find out what that was.

I opened my mouth, about to take it to the next phase, when he grabbed my arm and shook it. "Jill sent you, didn't she? That little bitch. She's not paying me, is she?"

"Take your hand off my arm."

He squeezed tighter, the cigarette dangling from his mouth.

"I said, take your fucking paw off me." My voice had steel behind it. Plan or no plan, I wasn't fond of being held down. Another ghost from my past.

"You're lucky I don't fuck you up. Then you can go show your black-and-blue face to Jill and let her see what's in store for her. And if I'm in the right mood, I might do the same to that cute little girl of hers. What's her name—Lila?"

I bit my tongue. It was either that or lose my shit on this guy.

That would blow everything, though, including my cover. I had to remain under control and not lose focus on the ultimate goal.

I shifted my eyes to his chest for a quick second, where I saw the red beam. I turned my head and put my hand up to my left ear. I said, "I was just told by Shock One that if you don't let go of my arm, he's going to fire a forty-caliber bullet into the middle of your chest."

"Do what?" He jerked his head around. "There's nobody else here except you and me." It sounded like he was questioning his own assessment.

"Look down at your chest."

He lowered his chin, then lifted his head and slowly removed his hand from my arm. "Who are you?" he asked.

"I could say something like, 'Your worst fucking nightmare,' but that would be too cliché. And I'm not sure you'd take it seriously."

I paused, crossed an ankle over my opposite knee. I'd transitioned from the poster child for extreme anxiety to Mrs. Cool.

"What's up with the sniper? Wait, are you working for one of my other clients from the north side? If so, I didn't mean to threaten their kids. It was a joke. Ha-ha." He showed me his yellow teeth. Again, I felt the urge to gag. However, I managed to stay the course.

"You're only partially right, Bennie. There is a sniper in the park—his code name is Shock One. But I have another one here too. He's not a fan of laser lights on his targets. He uses his naked eye. His fellow soldiers in Afghanistan called him Awe One."

"What the hell is this? I didn't do anything to deserve a hit on me. And you got two snipers here? This ain't a fucking war zone, lady. You can't just kill people for the fun of it."

I shifted my eyes to the swing set, where one of the seats swung slightly in the breeze. "Bennie, you need to tell me where Angel Bailey is."

I could hear his breath hitch. I flipped my sights back to him and glared into his red-rimmed eyes.

"Who?" he asked, looking off into the sky.

He was playing games, wasting time.

"Bennie, I'm not screwing around. We know that Jill gave you her daughter under duress when she needed a fix and couldn't pay off her drug debt. Where is Angel Bailey?"

He shifted in his seat. I watched his eyes searching the grounds, most certainly looking for a way to get out of this alive. He didn't know that he could simply get up and walk away. Perception was everything.

"Just so you know, Bennie, the guys in this park are not hired hitmen."

He narrowed eyes.

"They're doing it as a favor. To Gerald Bailey. He served alongside Shock One and Awe One in Afghanistan."

"Shock and Awe," he whispered.

I nodded. "They're close, Bennie. And they'd love to take you out."

He looked at his cigarette. "I'm going to wipe my face, okay? I just don't want anyone getting trigger-happy."

"I'd move very slowly if I were you."

He did. When he finished, his skin seemed to have turned a gray color.

"Just answer the question, Bennie, and you get to keep living your wonderful life. It's actually pretty simple."

"I can't."

"Why not?"

He put the palm of his hand against his eye. "Because I don't have her. Not anymore."

"What do you mean?"

His eyes searched the area and held up a hand. "Just tell your Shock and Awe guys to not shoot me, okay?"

I was seething, and I knew he could sense my anger.

"Jesus, lady, you've got to understand the situation I was in."

"What happened, Bennie?"

"I'm sure she's okay…" His voice trailed off, as if he couldn't convince himself of the notion.

I put my hand to my ear—as if I were listening to one of the snipers speaking to me. "Awe is asking if I can give him the green light to put a bullet through your kneecap."

"No, no, no…please, no!" He started wiggling like a kid sitting in church.

"Stop moving, Bennie, or they will shoot without asking."

He put his hands over his kneecaps. Then he noticed his cigarette was about to burn his fingers, and he tossed it to the ground. But he quickly returned that hand to his kneecap.

As if that would save his knees. I would have laughed if I wasn't so pissed off.

"Start talking, Bennie. Where is Angel?"

"She's not in San Antonio."

"I didn't ask where she wasn't. Where is she, and who has her?"

"I think she's up in Nevada."

"How did she get up there?"

"Look, this whole drug thing is a messed-up business. It attracts the wrong kind of people, let me tell you."

He was talking as though he didn't belong to that club. Whatever. I gestured with my hand for him to continue.

"I had bills to pay, just like anyone else. I was a little short on cash, and when the piper came to pay my supplier, he said he'd take another form of payment. One that wouldn't cost me a dime."

"You gave Angel to some stranger?"

Wincing, he nodded ever so slightly, as if he were bracing himself for a bullet between the eyes.

"Who...who did you give her to?"

"If I tell you that, he'll come after me and kill me."

I tilted my head. "If you don't tell me, you won't make it out of this park alive." The ultimate bluff.

"Okay, okay." He put a palm up to his eye. "All I know is, he calls himself Cadillac, and he runs some bar outside of Vegas."

"He's your fentanyl supplier?"

He nodded.

"Is this the first girl he's taken?"

He did something in between a shrug and a shake of the head. I took that as a "no."

Then he said, "You know prostitution is legal up there, right?"

"She's fifteen, Bennie. Fifteen years old!" I jumped up and backhanded him across the face. The edge of a fingernail caught flesh, and his face started to bleed. I could feel my chest surging with every breath. "You're fucking scum!"

"I know, I know." He started to cry. "Please don't kill me. Please..."

I took in a deep breath. "Is there anything else you can tell me about this Cadillac person?"

"Nothing." He stopped crying and rubbed his face. "There's a rumor going around that he occasionally will flip the girl...you know, like you would a house."

My eyes bugged out. *"What?"*

"He gets a girl, then turns around and sells her."

Like she was some kind of product. I thought my head was

going to explode. Angel might not even be in Vegas. She could be anywhere in the country, or the world. Who knew what this Cadillac person had done with her?

I looked at Bennie. "You're going to get up and walk out of this park. If I find out you've lied about anything, you'll be getting a visit from Shock or Awe when you least expect it. They've hunted *terrorists*, Bennie. They'll certainly be able to find your sorry ass, no matter where you try to hide. And if you ever threaten the Baileys again, you're as good as dead. You got it, Bennie?"

He nodded like his head was a jackhammer. "No problem. They'll never see me again. Can I go now?"

"Yes, but move very slowly."

Once he cleared the park, I went over and waited for Cristina to jump down out of the tree.

"Did you record all that?" I asked.

"Every damn word."

"Get it to Stan. Plus, I'm going to text you a picture I have of Angel."

"Where are you going? We've got that appointment with the school-district official."

"You take it. I trust you. I'm going to Vegas."

Twenty-Two

Alex

Oddly enough, on our trek back into Vegas—which included catching a ride with a woman who was celebrating her eightieth birthday by driving into Vegas to "party like she was twenty-one again"—we found a small hospital before we found a law-enforcement office.

I convinced Becca to go ahead and have a sexual-assault forensic exam, also known as a rape kit. She cried before, and then she cried after. But she received lots of hugs from Erin and me. Doctors also treated Erin's wound as best they could. They said she would need to see a reconstructive surgeon to avoid her having an enormous scar on her face. I bit back tears when they gave us that news. Strangely, Erin didn't get upset. She listened and appeared to be thinking through some things. I knew the demons would come back like acid reflux, not just over the next few days but well into the future, most likely. I planned on finding a counselor for her once we made it back home.

It took three hours before Erin, Becca, and I walked through the sliding glass doors of the hotel the Faulks were staying in. We'd called from the hospital to let them know we were on our way. We didn't provide details about the trauma Becca had sustained, or the murder, or any other horrors they'd witnessed. Sonya and Byron would have plenty of time to comfort their daughter and heal as a family.

Sonya and Byron spotted us from across the gold and red lobby. They sprinted in our direction and engulfed Becca in a family hug. Tears were shed, but also a lot of kisses and follow-up hugs.

"Prayers have been answered!" Sonya yelled, taking Becca's hands in hers.

"You don't look too bad. Maybe a little on the dirty side, but you weren't hurt or anything, were you?" Byron said, hitching up his pants.

Becca looked down at the colorful lobby carpet. Not surprisingly, the carpet had a motif of blackjack tables, slot machines, and dice. She seemed unsure how to respond. I thought his question was poorly timed and naïve. Maybe his brain just couldn't fathom her being harmed.

I spoke up. "There's lots to share, Byron, maybe when you guys are alone. But I will tell you that they escaped on their own. They actually just happened to stumble upon me in the middle of nowhere outside the city."

He walked over and shook my hand. "I can't tell you how grateful Sonya and I are for everything you did to bring our daughter back." He gave me the once-over. "You look about as dirty as the girls."

I shrugged. A moment later, Sonya wrapped her arms around me from the side—the odd angle crunched my shoulders.

"You're my hero, Alex," she said. "I'm so sorry that we gave you a hard time when this nightmare started. We were so worried…we didn't have control of our actions. Right, Byron?" She turned and looked at her husband.

He gave a tight nod. "Yeah. Very sorry, Alex." His tone was

business-like. It had been a while since I'd seen the Faulks. Maybe at one of the girls' tennis tournaments. Sonya had changed her hair color—what woman didn't do that at least a couple of times a year? Byron, though, looked different, as if he'd gone on some major diet. He was leaner, a little disheveled. His raccoon-eyes were so hollow, it was almost like looking right into his skull. I was certain that once I looked in a mirror, it might crack, so who was I to judge someone's appearance after going through this hell? Even if Byron and Sonya didn't experience the horrors themselves, they, like most parents, were probably crumbling to pieces, waiting to get an update. I was just happy to see everyone happy.

The high of the reunion was soon followed by sheer exhaustion. Relief, yes, but the fatigue was very real. My knees became wobbly and my hands jittered.

"What do you say we all get cleaned up, rest some, and then meet down here for a celebratory dinner?" Sonya said, putting her arms around both girls.

"Sounds like fun to me," Becca said.

"I'm game." Erin reached over and gave Becca a fist bump, then she turned to me. "You cool with that, Mom?"

"We need to talk to local FBI agents, and that could take some time. You and Becca will need to share everything with them, and I'll have a few things to tell as well."

Sonya said, "We certainly want these horrible people behind bars, don't we, Byron?"

"Of course." He scratched the stubble on his face as his eyes drifted off. He looked like he carried a lot of anxiety. I could relate.

I agreed that we'd try to meet up later for dinner, but I'd first try to reach the local FBI office. There were more hugs—none bigger than the one between Erin and Becca—and then we parted ways. That was when I realized I had no money, no ID, and no phone.

"What's wrong, Mom?"

I gave her the quick de-brief on our financial situation.

"Hmm," she said.

"Hmm, what?"

"Hold on." She started walking off.

"Where are you going?"

"I'm going to catch up with Becca and her parents. I'm sure they'll get us a room and pay for our meals while we're here. Then you can just pay them back."

She flipped around and headed for the elevators on the other end of the lobby. I could see the top of Sonya's frosted hair.

While keeping an eye on Erin as she zipped through the crowd, I waltzed over to the front counter.

"May I help you?"

A quick glance to see a female employee with a smile wider than my head.

"Well..." I paused to ensure I didn't lose Erin in the crowd.

"You're waiting on someone?" she asked in a perky voice.

"Kind of. I'm watching my daughter, making sure she isn't..." I couldn't say kidnapped. "Just want to make sure she reaches her friend."

"Well, are you going to check in, or is there something else I can help you with?"

"You mind if borrow your phone?"

She didn't respond, so I took another quick glance in her direction. She looked confused.

"Not your personal cell phone. Your landline. The one with the cord on it?"

"Right. Okay. Why?"

"Because I lost mine." Didn't need to get into the details.

She handed me the phone, and I dialed Brad's cell. The moment after he said hello—of course, he had no idea it was me—I could hear the emotion fill his voice. "Alex?"

"Yes, it's me," I said through a whimper.

"Thank God you're okay. But you're crying. Is Erin—"

"She survived. She and Becca both went through hell. I've been to LA and back, and had to deal with… I'm not sure I really want to relive the whole thing again. Not right at this moment."

He sighed. "That's fine, babe. I'm just so happy to hear your voice. I was up all night. I called Jerry and told him everything after he promised not to take action until I gave him the green light. But hearing that you're okay… You *are* okay, aren't you?"

"Now I am. Although I'd wished like hell that you were here about a hundred times in the last two days."

"I should have gone with you."

"You couldn't have. If they'd seen me with you, they would have probably killed you, maybe me too. Well, maybe not until after I did their drug run."

"Oh boy. This story sounds like it's one for the ages."

I looked up and saw Erin walking toward me.

"Every time I think I've come across the worst kind of humans, I find something even lower."

"I'm so sorry you had to deal with this on your own. You don't need to get into all the details, but are you or Erin physically hurt?"

"Nothing we can't get over. Becca, though…she was raped."

"My God. How is she dealing with it? How are her parents dealing with it?"

"Becca's doing okay for now. I'm sure she'll need some help. As for her parents, they don't know yet. We just walked into the hotel, had the joyous reunion, and then they went up to their room. So, Becca could be telling them right now."

"I want to fly out there and make sure you two get home safely and without any hassle," he said.

"I want you here now, dammit."

He chuckled.

"Seriously, I've got no energy. I'm completely drained. Erin and I would like to rest a while, get cleaned up, maybe have some dinner with the Faulks later."

"So, Sonya and Byron chilled out with their attitudes?"

"They were both ecstatic to see Becca. Sonya couldn't get the smile off her face. She apologized profusely. Byron sorta did too. He's an odd bird."

"Not a ringing endorsement of Mr. Faulk."

"Eh. He's a high-stress guy, I can tell. But the man has been through a lot. We all have."

"I'm glad you guys are in a good place. I mean, they kept accusing you... Hearing that, it was hard for me to stomach. It was nuts. I'm glad I don't have to come out there and defend my woman."

We both laughed at his caveman-like comment.

"You can do me a big favor, though."

"Your wish is my command," he said.

"Oh, we'll play that game when I get home. For now, I just need some money. Carter and Nixon destroyed my phone, took everything I had."

"Carter and Nixon? Was some president-impersonation group behind all this?"

"Eh. Something like that. More information later, like I said."

We worked through the details of him wiring me some money. Erin pulled up next to me just as I handed the phone back to the hotel employee, so Brad could book us a room and ensure the clerk understood that the highest levels of the FBI would appreciate the hotel's support by allowing us to check in while I waited on my money and ID.

"No can do," Erin said, glancing over her shoulder toward the elevators.

"I'm tired, Erin. What am I missing?"

"Oh, Mr. Faulk. They said they're a little strapped for money right now, and they wouldn't be able to help us out."

I stopped and stared at her. Was she kidding? Surely, the Faulks weren't *that* strapped. In fact, they should have offered. I closed my eyes and took a deep breath, willing myself to calm down. *Don't add to the stress, Alex.* I said, "No worries. I spoke to Brad, and he's talking to the nice lady now so we can get us a room. We'll be fine."

"Cool," Erin said. "I miss Brad. And Ezzy and Pumpkin."

"What about your brother?"

"Squirt? Yeah, I guess."

"Hate to break it to you, but Luke's gaining on you. He's not such a squirt anymore."

She waved a dismissive hand in front of her face.

The lady handed the phone back to me, saying, "I've got you taken care of. When you're done, I can show you the different cell phones that you can choose from."

"Oh, Mom, can I get the latest…?"

I held up a hand. "Cheap and easy. That's all we need."

"You're right." She smiled, put her head on my shoulder, and hooked her arm in mine.

I told Brad I'd text him my new cell number. He, in turn, would reach out to the local FBI office after talking to Jerry, who seemed to know someone in just about every government agency and office.

"I'll let you know our flight info for tomorrow whenever I book it."

"Let me do it," he said.

"Thank you. You're just what I need right now."

Brad and I both said, "I love you," and I felt that warm feeling inside.

Erin and I got our room key and headed upstairs. She said, "Have I ever told you that you're the best mom ever?"

"Not in this century, no." I winked at her.

"Well, you are."

My heart smiled until my head hit the pillow.

Twenty-Three

Ivy

I packed a bag while speaking to Saul on the phone.

"What did Stan say when you called him?" he asked.

"He called me after Cristina sent him the audio file of my interaction with Baldwin." I pulled a handful of socks from a drawer and tossed them into a duffel bag.

"Fine. And so…?"

"Said it would never hold up in court. Entrapment."

"Hmm."

"So you agree?" I asked.

"Without listening to it, I'd say it's a gray area. But I can see where he's coming from."

"So that's why I'm going to Vegas." I opened the closet, pulled three shirts off their hangers, and stuffed them in with the other clothes. "Well, honestly, I'd probably be going anyway."

"At least you're being honest." He sighed.

"I hope you're not angry with me."

"Just worried. I thought we were past all of this life-threatening drama."

"My life wasn't threatened."

"Only because you and Cristina fooled Baldwin into thinking

you had snipers taking aim at him. Damn, that guy is gullible."

"He's paranoid, just like most of his customers probably. Hell, you should have seen Jill. It was heartbreaking, but also sickening to hear what she'd done with Angel."

"Wait. Have you given her an update?"

"No way. Stan and I didn't talk long, but he did tell me that he'd started the process to get the charges against Gerald Bailey dropped so he could get home to take over for the CPS caseworker and care for Lila. That little girl is the person I'm second most concerned about in all of this."

"The first being Angel?"

"Yep. Stan also told me that he'd personally assist Gerald in making sure Jill was put in a detox center before the day ended."

"So you're really kind of doing this on Gerald's behalf. He's, more or less, your client."

"I know you're hinting that I'm doing pro-bono work again. But if he were able to talk to me right now, he'd hire me in a second. Stan said he'd tell Gerald what he'd heard on the audio and where I was headed. I know Gerald will pay me if I can bring his daughter home. But getting paid has nothing to do with why I'm going."

"I know, Ivy. That's why I love you. You have tremendous compassion."

"Maybe. I think it's driven by fear as much as anything else."

"You're afraid? I want to help."

"No, I'm not afraid. I'm pissed. But I'm afraid for Angel. Who the hell knows what this Cadillac guy is doing to her?"

I ran into the bathroom and scooped the essentials into a small plastic bag, then I put that into my duffel bag and left my apartment. My mind was already thinking about Las Vegas and how I could figure out who this Cadillac person was.

I heard some muffled voices on the line and realized Saul's

attention was elsewhere. "You still there?"

"Yeah, sorry. I'm trying to work with Kyra to figure out if we can move this deposition I have set up for tomorrow morning."

Saul's small firm consisted of two people—himself and Kyra, his legal assistant. While it hadn't been evident when I first met her, she was bright and brought a lot of positive energy to the office. Initially, though, I had my reservations. Mainly two of them. She looked more like Morgana the Kissing Bandit than a serious professional. Her experience in a work setting was limited to scooping ice cream. Had I been jealous? Hell yes. But Saul never gave me a single reason to feel inferior. Since then, Kyra had grown on me. She seemed to take her job seriously and learned to not flaunt her most obvious assets.

"Saul, it's okay, really. I can handle this one. I'll be fine."

"When have you ever said otherwise?" he asked.

He had a point. "Okay, but you and I know there's no monster out there trying to hunt me down. This is about finding a scared teenaged girl who—"

"Who could be in danger." A slight pause. "I want to go with you, Ivy. We could make a hell of a team."

I couldn't see it, really. Saul was my perfect partner in so many ways, but I wasn't sure I wanted him to witness my on-the-job intensity on a close-up basis. Before I could further calm his fears, he continued. "I don't know if I can pull off moving tomorrow's deposition, Ivy, now that we're looking at this lawsuit I'm working. It's the biggest case I've ever had. I'm representing the plaintiff in a whistleblower case against a big gas company called Glory Hole, and I have a deposition with the executive vice president of HR."

"Glory Hole?" I snapped off a laugh.

"I know, lots of jokes on that name." He let loose a loud exhale. "Look, it might be my biggest case, but nothing is more important than your safety. So, I'll drop everything and come with you. There will be other cases."

"Don't you fucking dare drop the case. I'm a grown woman. If I needed you—and you know I'm not really fond of using that word, 'need'—but if I did, I'd ask."

"Okay, you don't *need* me. Maybe you would enjoy my company. We could play strip poker in our hotel room."

I smiled, but then I thought about who else was in Saul's office. "Hey, is Kyra standing right there?"

"No, she stepped out to the receptionist area to take another call."

I felt stupid for asking. "Look, if it makes you feel any better, Stan said he would call his cousin Nick, the one with the FBI, and—"

"I know Nick, silly."

"Okay, then. So, Stan is going to share this audio recording with Nick and see if he thinks the FBI can do anything with it."

"Good idea, although Nick's in the Boston office. Not sure that does you a lot of good in the next few hours in Las Vegas."

"Don't worry. I'll stay in touch with you."

My phone beeped as I got into Black Beauty. I told Saul I'd call him later and then I punched up the line. "Okay, Cristina, I'm going to need a little bit of your time."

"When you say a little, that means a lot. You know that, right?"

Never thought about it. Didn't have time to think about it. "We need to find out who this Cadillac person is and where I can find him in Las Vegas."

"*We* as in *me*?"

"I can try to do some research on the plane if you're too busy."

"You never asked me about the meeting with the school-district official."

I had to remind myself that Cristina was still only nineteen and, at times, needed a pat on the back, or at least some acknowledgment of her hard work. Hell, we all needed that.

"Okay, how did the meeting with the school-district official go?"

"Bottom line, we got the gig."

"Nice. You won them over with your effervescent charm, I'm sure."

"Effer— What the hell does that mean? Don't tell me. I didn't charm anyone. I just asked what she needed and told her we could do the background checks."

"Cool. Thank you."

She made a scoffing noise. "Well, I guess you get some of the credit. You'd already filled out all of their forms and talked to her on the phone. So…"

"Did she give you a date by when they need all of them completed?"

"It's on some type of schedule, a certain percentage done every week. I think they're giving us a month in total, but we can't screw around for three weeks."

She sounded like the boss. I appreciated her responsibility. "We can hit that timeframe."

I heard her clear her throat. She was thinking I wouldn't be around to help. "I won't be gone long, Cristina. At least I hope not. I just have to find Cadillac and hope and pray he still has Angel. If he doesn't, then I probably can't do anything more. I'll just have to hope we can get the Feds to take ownership of the investigation by then."

"I guess I won't ask which one has the higher priority, the background checks or searching for Cadillac," Cristina said.

"You know the answer. And you've got about five hours to find Cadillac. I know you work quickly on your phone. But this could be a challenge, even for you. You up for it?"

"Get the hell off my line. I've got work to do."

She ended the call before I could say another word.

Twenty-Four

Alex

Erin and I both took showers, changed into clean clothes that we'd purchased with the cash Brad had wired us, and then we flopped onto the bed. After a few minutes of talking, silence took over the room. My eyes grew heavy, and I fell asleep.

***

Erin nudged my shoulder. "Your phone is buzzing." Her voice sounded like Demi Moore, as if she were hoarse.

I moved to one elbow, rubbed an eye, and patted the bed, looking for the phone. "Seems like I've only been asleep for thirty minutes."

"We have," Erin said as I found the phone and punched up the line.

It was the local FBI agent in charge of this new investigation. My first thought: Brad and Jerry had moved fast. Maybe too fast, seeing how wiped out Erin and I were. But it was nice someone was finally taking control.

We agreed to have one session with the FBI agent, Dan Tanner, this evening, and then another follow-up session tomorrow morning. I learned he was also lining up interviews with the Faulks.

Erin texted Becca, and we agreed to meet the Faulks for dinner at the steak restaurant in the hotel after round one of our interviews tonight.

Erin and I tried to fall back asleep after the call, but Erin asked if she could talk to me. I sat up, and she started sharing what she'd felt during her captivity, how she'd prayed for the chance to get back to doing normal things. Things that she may not have appreciated much in the past, like going to her trigonometry class, attending pep rallies, hanging out with her brother. She felt like the kidnapping would totally change her outlook on life.

I didn't talk much as she was sharing. I nodded, reached over and touched her knee. I could sense her need to just dump everything out there. The order of her thoughts wasn't chronological, and I completely understood why. She bounced back and forth between the incident and how her future life would be different. She spoke about how, at one point, when it seemed like she and Becca would never be released, a feeling of hopelessness had consumed her, at least for a few hours.

A tear bubbled in her eye.

"I'm so sorry I wasn't there for you, Erin."

"It's not your fault, Mom. It really isn't. I just need to, you know...." She reached over and snatched a tissue from a box.

"I get it. How did you make it through those hours when you were depressed and thought you wouldn't be able to leave?"

She sniffled and then released a deep breath. "Well, a couple of times, I wondered if I could break through a window and jump to the ground. I knew the glass might cut me up, but I thought I could run off and find some help. Maybe it would have worked; maybe it wouldn't have. But then I saw Becca, and she was so out of it. And I thought, *If I ran off...would they harm her?* So, I figured I needed to stick around and come up with something else."

Putting someone else's needs before hers. Damn, she'd grown up a lot. I just wish it hadn't come out through an incident like this. Then again, she'd already shown signs of being selfless during times of stress. I looked at the cut on her face. Tears welled in my eyes, and I said in a soft voice, "You make me proud to be your mother."

She handed me a tissue. "Come on, Mom—don't get mushy on me now," she said with a quick giggle.

She went on to share that she saw so many other girls who were close to her age and how they looked like skeletons with hollow eyes. I told her I saw the same thing for the few minutes I'd walked the main hall of the compound.

"I hope your FBI people here in Vegas can find them before Carter does something worse to them."

"Me too."

We washed our faces and met Tanner and another FBI agent in the lobby. They'd already secured a hotel meeting room where they would conduct the interviews. A camera was set up in the room. Tanner's partner, a shorter guy, did all the legwork. He brought each of us into the room, made sure the camera was working, and then would slip out to prep the next person to be interviewed. They started with Sonya Faulk, and then talked to Byron, Becca, and Erin. When my daughter came out, she looked tired.

"You doing okay?" I asked.

"I can tell I'm not going to enjoy having to tell this story over and over. But if it can help the girls who are still being held…"

I nodded. "Exactly. I'll be out in a minute. Stay close to the Faulks until I'm out."

She gave me a mock-salute—which reminded me that her spirit hadn't been broken. I loved it.

Agent Tanner and I shook hands when I walked into the interview room. He said his boss used to live in Boston and apparently knew Jerry from back in the day.

I said, "I'm not surprised."

Tanner looked like your generic agent. No real accent, so I guessed he was from the Midwest. Dark hair parted on one side. He wore a blue sports coat and a collared blue shirt. The only thing that stood out was a small scar under his right eye.

At least his was visible.

I shared my story, starting with the phone call from the person with the digitally altered voice. I pointed out the difference between my call and the call the Faulks received. He put his hand to his chin. He didn't take notes. He had the fancy video recorder if he wanted to go back and check the stories.

I moved on and told him about being mugged the first time in a trailer. I gave him the location.

"Not a good part of town," he said.

"I learned that the hard way."

"Something tells me you would have gone anyway."

"Do you have kids?" I asked, trying not to sound defensive.

"Two. Ages nine and eleven."

I opened my palms to the ceiling. He didn't respond, but he seemed to get my point—he nodded and pursed his lips together.

Eventually, I reached the part of waking up in the hallway of the compound, my mind in a dizzy haze. I shared what I saw in the rooms—all of it. And then how I ran right into the large man who wore the Richard Nixon mask. From there, I explained my thoughts on Carter—the one likely in charge—with his Eastern European accent and metrosexual habits and high-end jeans.

Tanner nodded again and asked me to continue. I explained

my journey to south LA, where I came face to face with another deviant, Grant Valdez, who, apparently, was Carter's inside guy with the US Customs and Border Patrol. I told him how I'd escaped with the boxes and headed back to Vegas.

So far, Tanner didn't have much to say. He was listening but had no expression at all, really. He either wasn't surprised, or he was bored. The vibe I was picking up didn't give me the sense that the bad guys better run and hide. In fact, they might be out by the hotel pool having cocktails, and Tanner might, at some point, figure it out and arrange a time to talk to them.

I took in a deep breath and realized my well of cynicism runneth over. Tanner was probably just maintaining a professional demeanor. Still, I decided, for the moment, to leave out my interaction with Officer Bruce Massey of the California Highway Patrol. The guy had been embarrassed enough. Why put him through another round that would likely lead to his firing?

I went on to tell Tanner about the last act of the saga: how I'd found the compound empty, how Nixon had jumped my car battery and then changed vehicles at the gas station. I tried my best to pinpoint the location for Tanner. Then I talked about Nixon leading me to a trailer far off the main road. I described the ensuing fight with Nixon, how Carter stole the car with the drugs in it, and then ultimately how Nixon died.

"And a few minutes later, I heard Erin's voice." My voice cracked on the last couple of words.

He nodded, still showing no emotion. He reached for the door, then turned to me and said, "You never told me where you got the gun from."

Crap. The gun. Think fast, Alex. "I saw it on the floor when I ran out of Valdez's house. I grabbed it, thought it would come in handy at some point."

"That was convenient…that he just left a pistol sitting on the floor."

"The guy's a real winner," I said. "Who knows where he got the gun from or what other illegal activities he has going on?" I knew my white lie might come back to bite me in the ass. Then again, I didn't have an abundance of confidence that Tanner would really dig into the details of this investigation. I doubted he would ever talk to Valdez.

Tanner moved his head from side to side, as if he were contemplating my story, ninety-nine percent of which was the truth.

"So, are you going to send out a team to the compound? I'm sure Erin and Becca told you about the dead girl they saw get buried behind the shed."

He shut off the camera and started packing up. "We're in the interview phase right now. You guys are safe, and that's important. But, yes, I'm sure we'll send some people out there and try to verify your statements."

Verify our statements? Both of my palms dropped to the table. He snapped his eyes in my direction.

"I'm aware that prostitution is legal in regulated brothels, but I'm sure you can tell by our statements that none of this was normal. They kidnapped my daughter and her friend. Becca was raped, drugged…there are countless other girls in the same situation. It's basically a sex-drug prison. The value of the drugs in my car, I'm almost certain, was seven figures."

"I thought you never looked in the boxes?"

"I didn't, but all signs indicate that I was being forced to be a drug-runner. Think about it—they have a guy on the inside at CBP who receives packages from overseas, and then they get people like me, with everything to lose, to bring the drugs to them. They were going to kill me. Who knows how many parents like me they've killed? But right now, there are many girls who need our help. They're being used and abused by these...these monsters." My voice was pitching higher with every sentence, it seemed. I could feel my jaw twitching.

Tanner loaded the camera in a satchel. "Agent Troutt, you're very personally involved in this incident, so I understand your emotion. Just know that here in Las Vegas, in Nevada in general, we've worked out a relationship with the, uh, *other side* of the law to where we can all coexist in a peaceful way. Those who don't follow our unwritten rules or who cross the line...of course, they need to be brought to justice, like maybe these people who harassed you and the girls."

"Harassed?" My voice bounced off the walls.

He held out a hand as if I should calm down. I tried not to grab it and break two fingers.

"Nevada is unlike any other state in the country. It used to be a lawless place years ago. But now that we all know the role we play, tourism for everyone, families included, has made this a wonderful destination. So, I'm just saying it takes a more nuanced approach than just running around with guns blazing."

I got out of the chair and walked to the door. "*That's* your reaction after listening to our statements, huh?"

"It's just different here. I didn't create the rules, but I do know how to get things done and not turn the world upside down."

"I'm glad I know now," I said, opening the door.

"Know what?"

"That you're an embarrassment to the Bureau and a worthless piece-of-shit agent."

I slammed the door behind me and went to go eat dinner.

Twenty-Five

Alex

I stepped into a space of the hotel lobby where it smelled like cherry, as if I'd been dunked into a canister full of maraschino cherries. I assumed this was another trick of the casino trade—to make it more inviting for tourists to spend money. The inside of my cheeks tingled, and I started salivating.

"Mom, your face is, uh…classic."

I must have been making a face too. "Classic, huh? Is that supposed to be a compliment?"

Erin curled her arm inside of mine. "Sure, if you want it to be."

I guided us a few feet closer to the sliding glass doors. There was a glare from the midday sun, but the brief moments of fresh air every time the doors opened was a nice respite. We were waiting on the Faulks to say goodbye. Agent Tanner had called earlier and said he didn't need to interview us a second time. For some reason, that didn't surprise me.

"You know," Erin said, as we watched three young women walk into the hotel, holding their shoes in one hand and their bras in another, "the hotel is only trying to cover up the cigarette smell."

"I know," I said, waving a hand in my face. It seemed like the cherry odor was embedded in my nose. Off in the distance, we could see the same girls stumble onto the elevator. It was rather obvious they'd been out all night.

"Don't worry—you'll never see me doing that. I've had all the growing-up experiences a person can take," Erin said.

I felt like she actually believed what she said. I wanted to believe it too. But deep down, I knew Erin would probably hit that age when she'd want to experiment in a lot of areas. In a couple of years, she'd be off to college—the breeding ground for experimentation. Looking back to my college years, I was damn lucky to be alive. I'd gone to the University of Texas in Austin for undergrad. Enough said about that period of life. I felt pretty certain this latest incident would shape Erin's life, though. Hopefully for the better, and without making her paranoid.

A man wearing sunglasses and a cap for the new NHL team in town, Las Vegas Golden Knights, walked in the door. He took a final drag of his cigarette and blew it in our direction.

"Excuse me," I said.

He didn't hear me. Probably for the better.

"Reminds me of Mr. Faulk last night." Erin scrunched up her nose but then quickly touched the gash on her face. I tried not to reach out and touch her as if she were a five-year-old. But I just wanted to wipe the pain away, inside and out.

"Yeah, all those times I'd seen the Faulks at the tennis tournaments, I had no idea he was so over the top...well, about everything. I think if I'd known that about him, I probably wouldn't have let you go on this trip."

She turned slightly, but I still caught her rolling her eyes. Then she flipped around and faced me. "You know this has nothing to do with Mr. Faulk being a drunk, right?"

I held up two hands. "I know, I know. Don't you think his

behavior was way out there?"

"Let's just say it. He got shitfaced. Becca tells me it happens all the time. Well, in the last few months."

"Have you ever seen him act like he did last night?"

Last night had been a sight to behold. By the time Erin and I arrived at the table, Byron had ordered two bottles of champagne, one for himself and one for Sonya and me to share. I ended up drinking half a glass. Sonya might have had a full glass. Hard to remember, because all eyes were on Byron.

He stood up half the time, as if he were holding court…like he couldn't control himself. He was attempting to do card tricks at the table. At first, his tricks and tipsy, jovial demeanor were almost humorous. But the more he drank, the nastier his comments became. Then came the cigarettes. He took chain-smoking to another level, lighting up two at a time. Then he started doing shots. The more he smoked, the more he drank. Which led to cruder comments to anyone within earshot.

It was a vicious and ugly cycle that went on far too long. Sonya and Becca both seemed embarrassed by the episode. I finally had enough and told everyone that Erin and I were headed up to our room. For some reason, Byron thought it was the perfect time to compare his wife's body to that of one of the showgirls, who'd just walked by our table. I almost walked over and punched him in the jaw. A rush of unpleasant memories had lit up my brain like a firecracker show—back when my dad was a walking, talking drunk. Dad had embarrassed me more than once, but he was never that mean. Dad's biggest target of his derisive comments was himself.

"You mean, where he's cussing at everyone…nice one minute, mean the next?" Erin said. "Nope. I've seen him drink a lot. I've read about functional alcoholics, and that's what I thought he was. But Becca, during our time together walking those hills, shared something with me."

She pressed her lips shut and looked over her shoulder. No sign of the Faulks yet. We'd give them another ten minutes, and then we'd have to head to the airport.

I tried not to let my imagination run wild during the few seconds I waited for Erin to continue. She had gone through too much. Becca had been sexually assaulted. It was all I could do not to think about putting Erin in a convent when we got home.

She bit her lower lip, as if she were still mulling over what she should say. "So, I'm kind of breaking a friendship oath right now," she finally said, again glancing over her shoulder.

"It's okay, Erin. I'm not going to run off and post something on Snapchat."

"Well, duh! I know that. But it's more about me...you know, not breaking the trust with my best friend."

"I get it." I held it at that, hoping she'd continue. She did.

"Becca told me they almost lost their house a month ago."

"What? I thought both her parents had jobs...*good* jobs. Isn't she an assistant principal at the elementary school, and he's a CPA, right?"

"Yeah, I guess. But does it really matter what job you have if you spend too much money?"

Erin was showing some youthful wisdom.

"Solid point, daughter. So, they were able to keep the house, apparently."

"But only because Becca's grandparents came in at the last second and paid their mortgage."

My eyes looked past Erin to see the Faulks walking in our direction from the elevators. Not surprisingly, Byron had on sunglasses and his hands were buried in his pockets.

"So you think everything's okay now?" I asked Erin.

She shook her head. "Becca hears her parents fighting all the time. She thinks it's usually about money, although she asked her mom about it and she said they were fine, their financial situation was fine. Everything was fine."

I nodded. "The great equalizer."

"Why do you say that?"

"When someone says it's never about the money, it's always about the money."

She shook her head as if she wasn't following me. "Like with what?"

"With everything."

"Never knew you were so wise, Mom."

"Thanks."

"I always knew you were badass, though." She smirked.

"Better to be a dumb badass than not a badass at all."

She giggled. "You're funny when you cuss."

I popped an eyebrow for Erin, and then the Faulks walked up and we all said our goodbyes. Byron and Sonya acted as though nothing had happened last night. Should have predicted as much, given my experience in such matters. The worst drunk is always the one with the convenient loss of memory. Erin and Becca giggled and talked like they hadn't seen each other in a week. I smiled and hoped that Becca would get the help she needed once they traveled back to Salem.

"So, are you guys heading out later this evening?" I asked.

"You kidding me? I got us tickets to a big boxing match tonight," Byron said, his voice sounding like he was gargling pebbles.

I glanced at Sonya. Her eyes looked to the ceiling. That spoke volumes. A month ago, the guy had no money to pay the mortgage. Yesterday even, they told Erin they couldn't loan us some money so we could get a room for the night.

It just hit me. We were in the mecca of gambling. That was

probably at the heart of Byron's issues. He'd gambled away all their money. Big winner one day; big loser the next. And in there somewhere, he'd drink himself into oblivion. I felt even sorrier for Becca. As for Sonya, I had empathy as well. Then again, she could be enabling his behavior.

I was ready to get the hell out of Vegas, though, and that included steering clear of the Faulks. We waved goodbye one last time as we crawled into a cab and headed for the airport.

Twenty-Six

Alex

During the ride, Erin and I stayed quiet, each of us looking out our windows at all the casinos. I recalled the feeling I had when I'd flown into Vegas. Acid had nearly ripped a hole in my stomach lining. But now I had my daughter safely with me, and we were going to go home to reunite with our own family. Brad and I wanted to show the kids and Ezzy a couple of the houses we'd looked at. He and I had talked last night. I finally told him all the details of what had happened. He was a great listener, but it only made me want him by my side that much more.

Carrying only a backpack, I guided Erin to the back of the line for the ticket counter to pick up the tickets Brad had reserved for us. My phone dinged—I'd forgotten to put it on mute. It was a text from Nick, my once and future partner. He'd suffered severe internal injuries from a series of bombs during the Boston Marathon and just in the last week had returned to the office. He still hadn't been cleared to work in the field, so he was stuck in the office doing investigative work behind the scenes—an activity that made him quite grumpy. I read his text.

Take a look at this picture. Show it to Erin, and then call me.

Before I opened the picture, Brad sent a text.

Hey, Nick's sending u a text. Call me before you decide.

Decide what? I tapped on the picture Nick sent. It was a girl, maybe a little younger than Erin. She had a headful of dark curls. Her big smile was all braces and cheeks.

"What are you looking at, Mom?" Erin peered around my arm before I could decide if I wanted her to see it.

"It's just a picture that Nick sent me." I paused, wishing I had more information from Nick or Brad or someone. Too late now. "Does she look familiar to you?"

She took the phone from my hand and examined the screen. She looked up, stared off into the distance, and then turned back to the phone. Slowly, her mouth opened, and she said, "I'm almost certain this is the girl I saw in the other room."

A chill swept through me. "What girl? What room?"

"Oh, I didn't tell you?" She put a fingernail in her mouth.

I shook my head.

"Crap. I never mentioned it to that FBI agent guy, either."

Not sure that would have made much of a difference. "Talk to me, Erin. I don't know why Nick sent this to me. I'll call him here in a moment, but what did you see?"

"It's what I *heard* that got me to look through the crack of the door. I was upstairs using the restroom, and I heard this girl screaming. I couldn't help but look. When I did, I saw Carter standing there laughing as this other guy had her by the hair, jerking her back and forth like she was some stuffed animal. I thought he was going to rip her scalp off."

"So, Carter had on his mask?"

"All the time. I think he was paranoid."

"What about this other guy?"

"Pretty big guy. Maybe in his forties. Dressed like a biker with big boots, cut-off sleeves. Had one of those goatees that hadn't been trimmed in, like, forever. He was laughing too. It gave me the creeps. Then again, it was about the hundredth thing at the compound that gave me the creeps."

The airline employee behind the counter called for next in line. Erin and I walked up and gave them our names. Of course, I didn't have a driver's license, so this, initially, started a bit of an uproar. But then the man checked the reservation and spoke to his manager. Like I'd expected, Brad and Jerry had ensured we would have no problems getting through.

The man handed us our tickets and said we could bypass the normal security line. Erin and I stepped over to the side, and I asked her to hold up while I called Nick.

"What do you think is going on, Mom? Why would Nick send you this picture?" Erin asked.

I had the phone up to my ear. "No idea. Give me a—"

"Alex. Thanks for calling."

"Hey, Nick. That picture you sent. Erin thinks—"

"I know it's her, Mom," Erin called out.

"Actually, Erin is *certain* she saw that girl at the compound. Wait, you may not know everything that's gone on. A lot to catch you up on."

"I know it all, Alex. I talked to Brad. He told me everything. It's just…well, I'm so relieved that you have Erin back safely. And her friend?"

"Well, she's physically okay. But she was sexually assaulted. Erin has a pretty big gash on her cheek. We'll have to a see a surgeon about it. But they were lucky."

"You were too, from what Brad shared. I'm just sorry I couldn't be out there to help. This damn body of mine is getting better, but I'm not quite ready to take you on in a race."

He'd been challenging me to a race ever since he got out of the hospital—well, actually, I'd been the one to challenge him, but he wouldn't let it go. It seemed to motivate him during his rehabilitation, though. "Honestly, Nick, I could have used you. So, just know that you're missed, and we can't wait to have you back in the field. But let's talk about this girl. Erin saw her at the compound. She was being tossed around by some biker-looking guy. Not sure what happened to her and where she is now, though. I'm not sure if she was given to the guy running the compound, some drug-trafficking guy we call—"

"Carter. I know. I've been all over this since Brad filled me in. I heard about you being forced to be the drug-runner to get Erin back. Not to get into all the details, but I caught wind that the DEA is investigating some type of insider drug connection with the CBP. I have a call into them right now to let them know what happened with you."

"Great. Thank you. I'm not sure the local FBI agent here is going to do much. So, back to the girl. What do you know about her?"

"Well, I got the tip from my cousin Stan. You know, the San Antonio police detective."

"Nick, I just saw the guy a little more than a month ago. Of course I know Stan. Is this girl from San Antonio?"

"Just outside of the city, a place called Seguin."

"I've driven through there."

"Right. Your Texas roots. Well, this story is gut-wrenching. The girl's name is Angel Bailey. Her mom is an addict. Fentanyl—the most lethal opioid out there. She basically traded her daughter to her dealer to pay off her drug debt and allow her to keep getting more pills. It's just hard to believe what some people will do."

The air left my lungs in a rush. How could a mom do that? That was my initial reaction, and then I thought about it some more: addiction. I'd read somewhere that fentanyl was at least fifty times more potent than heroin. I blew out a breath. "So, you're calling me for a reason."

"Look, I know you've been through hell the last few days. You and Erin are at the airport?"

"Yeah. So?"

He sighed. "I hate to ask you this, but Stan's friend, Ivy Nash, is hell-bent on finding this girl."

"So, she's the one who found out about her situation?"

"Long story, but yeah. And she's the type of person who, if she grabs hold of something—especially a case involving a kid—she won't let go."

"I've never met Ivy in person. But remember, I was on a few conference calls with her a while back. She's…uh, tenacious."

"Good word. But she won't take a step back and let law enforcement do their work. I've made a call to the local FBI office. But Stan is asking for a favor."

He paused, so I finished his thought. "He wants me to try to find Angel and make sure Ivy doesn't get herself into trouble."

"Man, I feel bad even asking. You just got Erin back, and you probably can't wait until you get her home and start living a normal life again."

For a brief moment, I wondered what normalcy felt like, at least for an extended period of time. I looked at Erin, who was rocking back and forth on her heels, just doing some people watching. She seemed carefree, which was remarkable. I knew she had some things to work through, but she would get through it. She was strong, supported by her family and friends. Which then led my thoughts back to Angel. Who was protecting her? I instantly understood Ivy's motivation.

"Is Jerry aware of all this?"

"I filled him in. And he didn't squash it."

"You know I have no weapon, and I have no FBI creds on me."

"I figured. Listen, it's probably asking too much. I mean, Ivy was bullheaded and just took off."

I felt a hand on my shoulder. I turned around to see Erin looking at me. She said, "Nick wants to see if you'll help find the girl?"

I nodded.

"Then go do it, Mom. If anyone can find her, it's you. I'm worried sick about all those girls. If you can save this one, it would be awesome. Go do it. For me."

That was all I needed to hear. I put in a call to Brad to let him know my decision—he wasn't surprised. I got permission to walk Erin to the gate. I hugged her long and hard just before she boarded. And then I started my new assignment.

I only hoped that Angel was still alive to be saved.

Twenty-Seven

Ivy

With the sun beating down on me and vultures flying in a circle overhead, I took hold of the tire iron and pulled up one final time to tighten the last lug nut on the spare tire of my rental car.

"Pain. In. The. Ass." I wiped sweat off my face and then looked at my hands, which were mostly black from changing a tire in the middle of Nowhere, Nevada. I was sure my face now matched my hands. The last twenty-four hours had been brutal. I'd booked my flight without any problem—the airline made it easy to give them my money. After I went through security, the flight was delayed one hour. Then another hour. We finally boarded three hours after the original time. We were in the air for maybe an hour, and then the captain came over the loudspeaker saying we had to make an emergency landing in Odessa. Yes, Odessa—an absolute wasteland in West Texas. The only thing it was known for was Permian High School—the basis for the book, movie, and TV show *Friday Night Lights*.

I ended up sleeping in a plastic chair in the Odessa airport. I finally got a flight out earlier this morning. I grabbed the rental car, and now this…a flat tire. What would Cristina say if she were here? *"Pain in the fucking ass."*

Hell yeah, it was.

I tossed the tire-changing equipment into the trunk and wiped my hands on the rug. Then, I hopped into the driver's seat, rolled down the window, and opened up Cristina's email that she'd sent last night. She'd apparently found her way into a number of message boards that included discussions of where to find fentanyl around Las Vegas. From there, she took some discussions offline as she subtly asked about a guy named Cadillac. Three people, after she mentioned his name, didn't respond. On her fourth try, she received a response, but it was vague. She'd pasted it into a text to me: *Cadillac has his hands in a lot of the whorehouses. Lots of bizness there.*

That was all I had to go on. I wondered, of course, if that was how he was using Angel. Maybe he would "rent" her out to one of the brothels, like a pimp of some kind. Thankfully, Cristina had sent me a list of known brothels in the area. I took another look at the map and knew the closest one was in Nye County about ten miles away.

I started to pull onto the highway—the blaring horn sounded like it was on top of me. I hit my brakes and literally jumped off the seat as an eighteen-wheeler swerved around me. Tires squealed. Smoke snaked from the pavement. The truck dipped left and then right, but somehow the driver kept the rig on the road.

Then I heard the horn again. He held it down for a good thirty seconds as he drove away, blending in with the vaporized horizon.

I finally let out a breath. "Damn." My shoulders relaxed, and I wiped my eyes, even though I knew it was only smearing the black around.

"Where's my phone?" I asked aloud. I looked around me on the seat, on the floorboard. Nothing. I got out of the car so I could inspect the small space between the seat and the side of the car. That was when I saw it. The phone was lying on the road. I must have spastically tossed it out the window. *Good gosh, I'm a frickin' mess.*

I walked over and picked up one piece of it. The phone was trash.

Have you ever had one of those times when everything you do just turns to shit? Everything from the last twenty-four hours, culminating to now, made me wonder if I'd made a too-quick decision about coming to Vegas and looking for Angel without waiting on law enforcement to take the lead.

Waiting. Angel may not have much time. She was only fifteen.

"Fuck it." I got in the car, hit the gas, and headed for the brothel in Nye County.

Twenty-Eight

Ivy

As the woman waltzed down the wooden staircase in a pink dress and what I was sure was a fake diamond necklace, the resemblance was uncanny. She approached me, held out a gentle hand.

"I'm Lady Di. It's nice to meet you."

Yep, I'd just met royalty—well, a brothel's version of royalty—at the Pussy Cat Club. The real royal family would not be pleased. Up close, even in subdued lighting, her makeup made her look like she was wearing a mask. When she spoke, hardly any other part of her face moved. And her eyelashes reminded me of the drying flaps at the end of a car wash—they were that big and thick.

As I introduced myself, her eyes shifted and stopped at different places on my face.

"I had a flat tire down the road. So, I'm a little dirty at the moment."

"We do have a higher-end clientele."

She was essentially telling me that I looked like a lowly pit-crew member. She touched my elbow and guided me to the corner of the enlarged foyer of this two-story mansion. It was decked out like an episode of *Downton Abbey*—lots of wood and fancy rugs and candles and even a Big Ben clock. I was about to open my mouth when I saw one of her clients walking out from a side corridor with a young woman on his arm. Dressed in jeans with holes up and down his legs and wearing a baseball cap with the logo of a homebuilder on it, he was telling some type of joke, while she nodded with a thousand-yard stare. He was shorter than the woman by a good three or four inches. Perhaps this was the only "date" he could get.

At the door, he turned and kissed the woman on the cheek. She cringed as if his lips were made from the quills of a porcupine. "I'll see you next week, Cilla."

Cilla. As in Priscilla, perhaps? I didn't ask.

Then, he took her in his arms and was about to go in for another kiss, as if this was the big moment in their relationship.

Lady Di cleared her throat—it didn't sound very Lady Di-ish. It sounded more like Prince Charles. My eyes were drawn to the fashionable pink bow around her neck. Lady Di shifted her head to the side, one quick nod. She was giving the man, the client, a warning. I have a feeling that extra kiss would have been allowed if it had been accompanied by cash.

The customer removed his hands as though Cilla's body had just caught fire. He quickly exited the Pussy Cat Club.

Lady Di and Cilla didn't speak, but they watched each other like two felines guarding their young until Cilla disappeared down the darkened hallway.

"So," Lady Di said, her hands clasped in front of her dress, "I was told you wanted to speak with the, uh…manager."

I couldn't bring myself to say "the Madame." So, "the manager" had seemed like the next best thing.

The lack of a phone put me at a severe disadvantage—that was where I had the picture of Angel. "I wanted to ask you about someone. But just know that I'm not trying to get you or your establishment in trouble. I'm just a concerned friend."

Lady Di dipped her head for a moment and reset her feet, but she didn't speak.

"I had a picture, but...well, it's not available right now. The girl is a little shorter than me. She has dark-brown hair, tight curls. She has prominent cheeks, and when she smiles, it lights up a room. Oh, and she wears braces."

She paused a moment, looking at the floor. I'd decided to ask about Angel first, instead of Cadillac. Asking about a drug-dealing sex-trafficker might very well end the conversation before I could even mention Angel.

The silence lasted more than a few seconds.

"Look, she's just a teenage girl. If she's here, you probably had no idea about her age. So, just know that I only want bring her home to her family."

"Come with me." She whirled around on a heel and marched down the hallway by the stairs. I followed. Just past the staircase, she whipped around, pushed me against the wall, and plowed her forearm into my neck—I gasped for air.

"Who sent you?"

Lady Di's voice had just dropped an octave. Was Lady Di a cross-dresser?

"I. Can't. Breathe."

She released some of the pressure, and I blew out a breath.

"Answer me. Who sent you?" Lady Di now sounded like Voldemort. And with the shadows crossing her face, she was starting to look like him too.

"I'm working for her family. Is she here?"

Moving like a ninja warrior, Lady Di snapped off her shoe, pulled on the heel, and produced a blade that shimmered from a light behind her. Who the hell was this woman-man? Not like any Madame I'd seen on TV or the movies.

"We don't like people who ask questions about our girls."

"Angel is only fifteen years old. You guys are supposedly legal, right? So, if you have someone underage working here, I figured you'd want to know. You want this place to stay open."

Her—his?—forearm pushed into my neck again. I couldn't breathe. I tried clawing at her arm. It was like clawing at a tree trunk. She brought the blade close to my face.

"I don't believe a word you're saying. Too many people are coming around here asking about girls. So, I'm going to make an example out of you and carve you up like a fucking turkey." She laughed, showing all her teeth and gums. Air wasn't reaching my brain. I began to reach for her eyes. All I could grab were her eyelashes—but that was enough. I didn't let go.

Then the blade flashed, and I closed my eyes. Suddenly, the pressure against my throat was gone. I opened my eyes to see someone spinning Lady Di around. I couldn't see who it was, but they landed a straight punch into Lady Di's jaw. She grunted. A sidekick into the side of her knee, and she tumbled to the floor. The person dropped a knee onto Di's side, and the blade hit the floor. The person grabbed the knife and put it to the Madame's neck, at the same time pulling down the pink bow.

"If you move, I'll slice out your Adam's apple for good."

The woman looked up at me. "Are you okay, Ivy?"

I knew that voice. That was Alex Troutt.

Twenty-Nine

Alex

The man in the pink dress didn't fight back. Then again, he didn't have an option, really. Not unless he wanted to see a lot more of his own blood.

"What...?" Ivy looked at me, shook her head, her arms splayed.

She was asking what I was doing there. "Later. Are you okay?"

Ivy touched her neck. "I'll live."

I turned my sights back to this person who kind of looked like Lady Diana. *Crazy stuff.* "Why were you trying to hurt my friend?"

Lady Diana flinched, but I dug my knee into his stomach and held the blade at the tip of his nose. "You really want me to use your own weapon against you?"

He had on long eyelashes, lots of makeup. Even in the muted light, I could see his eyes cross.

"Who the hell are you?" Lady Di said. "A fucking ninja?"

"Doesn't matter. I asked you a question. Why were you threatening her?"

Ivy chimed in with, "Alex, this is Madame Lady Di. I was

just asking her, uh…him about a girl I'm looking for. Angel Bailey."

I gave a quick nod to Ivy, then went back to Lady Di. "So, what can you tell us about Angel? Does she, uh…work here?"

"No, and I told your friend that too."

"So, why did you pull this heel-knife on her?"

I heard shoes clapping against the wooden stairs above us.

"Would you mind if I stood up?" Lady Di said. "I don't want the girls to freak out. I'm not running anywhere."

I paused a second, trying to read his face. It was impossible. He wore so much makeup he didn't look human. "Okay, but I keep the blade for now."

He sniffed, lifted his chin. "I guess I'll have to walk on one heel, but sometimes a lady has to make sacrifices, I suppose." His voice had suddenly pitched higher. He rose to his feet and adjusted the bow around his neck—which hid his Adam's apple. Clasping his hands in front of his pink dress, he said, "There." He was now back in full character.

A girl walked by, gave us a quick glance, but kept moving. She was wearing a negligee with a sheer robe.

Just after the girl passed, Ivy spoke up. "So, Angel, the girl I described, doesn't work here?"

"No."

That was a quick answer. I asked, "Did you see Angel's picture?"

Lady Di shook his head, and then I looked to Ivy, who shrugged. "My phone got crushed…right after I was almost hit by an eighteen-wheeler, which happened after I got a flat tire."

I just shook my head. "One of those days?"

She rolled her eyes and crossed her arms. "Don't get me started."

I pulled out my phone, found the text from Nick, and showed

Angel's picture to Lady Di. "She could be using a different name," I suggested.

Lady Di studied it for a second. "Like I told your friend, she's not here. I don't hire girls who wear braces, no matter what their age is. And I don't hire underage girls. I don't want to be shut down. This place is a cash cow."

Ivy and I shared a quick glance, and then I swung my sights back to the Madame. He batted his eyelashes—they were the size of a bat's wings, although the ones over his left eye were only partially attached.

"Do you know anyone named Cadillac?" I asked.

The eyelashes stopped flapping; in fact, Lady Di might have stopped breathing. "I've seen Cadillacs in our parking lot," he said with a giggle that tried to be feminine but seemed to be hijacked by his real voice. I read that as stress.

"And I've seen Cadillacs on commercials, the ones with Matthew McConaughey. Don't play games with me."

"He does Lincoln commercials, thank you very much. Believe me, I follow that dreamboat in whatever he does." Lady Di popped an eyebrow. Who knew that it could move?

"Okay, whatever. I'm asking about a person named Cadillac."

He pursed his lips, as his eyes dropped to the floor. He knew something, but he was delaying.

I said, "Lady Di, or whatever your name is, you need to tell us where we can find Cadillac. We think he's kidnapped a girl."

No immediate response.

Ivy stepped a foot closer to Lady Di. "You *do* know that she's an FBI agent, yes? And she can shut down your cash cow faster than you can say 'Pussy Cat Club.'"

Damn, I wish she hadn't said that.

Lady Di got stiff and looked right at me. "Where are your

credentials? Is this some type of sting operation? I know my rights."

I rolled my eyes. "This is not a sting operation. We're not here to shut you down…not unless you don't cooperate."

He opened his palms to the ceiling. "I already told you that this Angel person does not work here. I've never seen her."

"I asked about Cadillac. Who is he, and where is he?" The runaround was getting old. I could feel stiffness in my neck.

He lifted his chin. "I need to see your FBI credentials. I know how this works. Too many people barge in here—earlier this morning even—acting like they're so important, throwing out threats left and right. I used to shudder every time that happened. No more. That's why I take a different approach now," he said, nodding at the blade in my hand.

He had anger-management issues, obviously. Then again, I'd never been in his…uh, her shoes. I wished, though, that Ivy had never gone there with the FBI comment.

"My credentials were stolen," I said.

He narrowed his eyes.

"What?" Ivy squeaked.

"It's a long story. Everything I have was stolen," I said to Ivy. Then I shifted my eyes back to Lady Di. "This Cadillac person may be connected to what happened to a family member of mine. So, while I may not have my FBI credentials on me, I'm one very pissed-off mother. You need to tell me everything you know about Cadillac. *Now.*" I didn't lift the blade, but I moved it around in my hand. Lady Di looked at it and then held up her hands.

"Cadillac isn't someone you want to screw with. If I say anything, and he finds out it came from my mouth, he might put his shotgun in my mouth and blow a hole through the back of my head." I heard a quake in his voice, which had returned to its natural octave.

"I hear you. But if we stop him, arrest him, then he won't threaten or harm you or anyone else."

He chuckled, but there was no humor behind it. "You don't understand. Cadillac has connections. Big connections. You don't get away with what he's done, or been rumored to have done, without knowing the right people. This is Vegas, baby. It's how the world works."

That sounded all too much like what Tanner had said. "Well, this is America, baby. We're not in some foreign country. It's illegal to kidnap girls, drug them, and use them as prostitutes."

He put a hand to his chest. "I would never..."

"But Cadillac would, right? And I'm guessing he's connected to the drug business in a big way."

He put a hand to his forehead. "Dear God, if this gets back to me..." He clipped off his sentence, pondering his next thought.

"You want to run a legal business with no hassles?" Ivy asked.

"Okay, okay. You can sometimes find Cadillac at the bar that he owns."

"The name?"

"The Wild Thing."

"The Wild Thing," I repeated under my breath.

"It has something to do with his career as a baseball player. Doesn't matter. Just please keep my name out of it." Lady Di's hands flitted around as he said this.

"You've been a great help." I nudged my head toward the front door. Ivy started in that direction, and I followed.

"Hey, what about my heel?"

"I'll leave it outside."

Ivy paused at the door, then turned back to Lady Di. "You said something about other people 'barging' in here. What did you mean? Were they asking about girls?"

"Three men were here earlier this morning, asking if I'd seen someone named Liv…Olivia Bradshaw, or was it Nancy? I'm not even sure I have the name right. I couldn't understand them very well, and they had a threatening presence." His voice trailed off for a second.

Ivy nodded. "And?"

"Probably nothing, but one of the Russians—"

"They were Russian?" I asked.

"I guess technically they could be from one of the former Soviet republics like Estonia or Latvia, but to get to my point, he said she could be with a younger girl."

"Why didn't you fucking tell us?" Ivy barked.

"Whoa, sister, back the fuck up. I didn't know—and I still don't know—who they were talking about."

"Did they show you a picture?"

"Of the younger girl? No. I just assumed it was like a little kid, maybe this other woman's daughter."

"But they showed you a picture of the woman?"

He nodded. "She was one of those trashy women who try too hard to shock you. Piercings all over her face, jet-black hair cut like she was a boy, and this crazy tattoo of a snake around her neck." His expression was pure revulsion.

I wasn't sure if these Russians were actually looking for Angel—my gut said no—but I reminded him that he'd find his heel blade in the parking lot.

"Just keep my name out of it. I want to live to see tomorrow."

I only hoped that Angel would as well.

Thirty

Ivy

Once outside, I found out Alex didn't have a car. She'd taken a cab from the airport after getting her ticket to fly out of Vegas.

"Fly out? When did you fly in?"

"Lots to share, but let's get out of this parking lot," she said, crawling into the passenger's seat.

I pulled onto the highway and started driving east. I felt her eyes on me.

"You're not what I pictured," she said.

She was referring to our previous interactions—all by phone. Almost two years ago, she was brought in to help me work a case that involved my best friend—well, the man to whom she was engaged, Zeke. Alex was in France at the INTERPOL headquarters as the lone FBI representative to work collaboratively on a plan to take down a drug-cartel leader based out of Ukraine. He was a former KGB agent. Alex had been invaluable in finding out whose team Zeke was really playing for. After watching my friend's father be killed right before my eyes, and then finding out my friend had been kidnapped, I had to have answers. Turned out, Zeke was somewhat of a double-agent, although nothing formal. He was a private contractor who was trying to do the right thing but was breaking countless laws in the process. He ended up saving my friend from sure death, and then he'd disappeared. Alex, though, had left an indelible impression on me. Even from across the pond, I felt she had this strength about her that seemed impenetrable.

"Must be the grime from changing the tire." I tried rubbing my face with my shirt sleeve.

She shook her head. "Not working."

"Thank you for saving my butt in there," I said.

"No problem. Your tax dollars at work," she said, arching an eyebrow.

"But you don't have your FBI credentials. I'm confused. I assumed you showed up because of the Stan-Nick connection."

"Yes...partially. There are two pieces to how I ended up here. The second part is much shorter."

She explained how Stan had sent the Angel photo and the recording of my conversation with Bennie Baldwin to his cousin Nick, who then, once he found out Alex was in Vegas, reached out to her asking if she'd assist.

"Well, I first asked my daughter if she recognized Angel, and she said yes."

"What the fuck? How would your daughter know Angel?" I asked.

"Well, that's the first part of the story." Her chest lifted, and she pushed out a long breath. And then she talked for fifteen minutes straight. By the time she finished, it felt like someone had taken a crowbar to my spine. I looked at her as she thumbed a tear out of her eye.

"I'm still a little emotional from it all."

"Jesus. I don't know what to say. I'm so sorry, but I'm also relieved that she's safe, and her friend too." I kept my eyes on a road that went straight as far as the eye could see. "Maggots like

Bennie Baldwin back in San Antonio and these perverts in the president masks and this Cadillac guy...that's why I started ECHO. No one really seemed to care about what was happening to young people. I couldn't just let these kids be abused over and over again. I felt like I had to at least try to make a difference."

"It's a great cause, Ivy. And you're a helluva strong woman to take it on."

I held up my fist. She kind of looked at it for a moment. "Don't leave me hanging," I said.

She chuckled and gave me a fist bump. "You're making me feel like I'm closer to Erin's age."

"Well, I work with an nineteen-year-old every day, so I guess it rubs off some."

"Cristina, right?"

I nodded. "So, you have no FBI credentials or a gun, and I have no phone."

"But you do have a car with a baby tire," she said.

"I guess that means no high-speed car chases."

She didn't respond. She was texting, although it was at a tortoise-like speed—the antithesis of Cristina. Her phone buzzed a minute later.

"Okay, while we wait for a text back from one of my colleagues, let me find out where this bar is. The Wild Thing," she said, pulling up a map app.

"So is that the plan? Just hunt down Cadillac at his bar?" I asked.

She was too focused to respond at first. Finally, she lifted her head. "I'm sorry. I'm getting too old to multitask. You were saying?"

"How do we find Angel? I mean, all I know is to go to every brothel in the area and ask about Angel or Cadillac. But we can see how well that went back at the Pussy Cat Club."

Her phone rang. "This could help us." She punched up the line and tapped the speaker button.

"Hey, Nick. I'm in a car with Ivy."

"Ivy Nash. How the hell are you doing?" Nick said.

"You don't want to know how my day's going. Alex tells me you're back to work and feeling better."

"Jerry, that sonofabitch, thinks I'm not ready for fieldwork yet."

I looked at Alex, who rolled her eyes and shook her head.

"I'm sure it will happen soon. Be patient, my friend," I said.

"Just remember, Stan and I come from the same gene pool. So, I don't like sitting on the sideline."

Alex jumped in. "Nick, what else have you found out about our boy, Cadillac?"

"Hey, Alex. Delmer Stratton is in the house. Whoop-whoop!"

My eyes went wide, and I mouthed *Who is that?* to Alex.

"Hey, Delmer. Thanks for jumping on."

She tapped the mute button and quickly said. "New guy on the team. Kind of annoying, very strange, but smart as hell. His father was FBI, and he died in the line of duty."

I nodded as Alex punched up the line again. "So, back to this Cadillac person, do we have any more—"

"This is my area of expertise, Alex," Delmer said.

"Okay, spit it out."

"Right here in the office, or should I go into the bathroom?"

"Seriously?"

"I'm just joking, Alex."

"A girl's life is on the line here, Delmer," I said.

"Oh, right. Ivy. Nice to meet you, Ms. Nash."

I gave Alex a cross-eyed look and said, "Hi, Delmer."

"Tell us what you know," Alex said.

"Cadillac was a relief pitcher. Spent most of his career at the

Triple-A affiliate of the New York Mets."

A pause.

"Okay..." Alex said.

"He had a decent earned run average, just under four, but he was all over the place. Lots of strikeouts—his fastball scared the crap out of most hitters. But lots of walks and hit batters. He had this evil laugh every time he plunked some batter on the elbow or knee. The guys who covered him always thought he had a screw loose."

"Great information, Delmer...if I was playing historical fantasy baseball."

"Technically," he said, "that wouldn't be possible since he was in the minor leagues. Although he had a cup of coffee with the Mets when he was in his late twenties."

I gave Alex a wide-eyed stare, and she held up her hand. I think she was saying this was part of the process of working with Delmer.

"You never said where he played his minor-league ball," Alex said.

"I figured you knew that the Mets' Triple-A affiliate is in Las Vegas, although they're in the process of changing teams. He played for the Las Vegas Stars. They've since changed their name to the 51s. Weird, right?"

I reached over and hit the mute button. "Weird is right. What isn't weird about this guy?"

Alex held up her hand again, nodded her understanding, and then reopened the line. "So, he's got a mean streak, and people think he had a screw loose. Good insight, Delmer."

"Why, thank you." He laughed, like a really "Goofy" laugh, as in the Disney character Goofy. "Let's back up a moment, though. What's his real name?"

"Damn, that should have been the lead. It's Travis Wild."

"The Wild Thing," I said in unison with Alex. We both smirked at our timing.

"You got it. Now you know how he came up with the name of his bar," Delmer said.

"Listen, kid…" Nick jumped in, but then I heard a groan. Maybe his injuries were still bothering him, even if he didn't want to admit it. "Can you get to the point on this guy?"

"Yes sir. So, Travis Wild has been arrested three times, but no convictions."

"Must have had a good lawyer," Alex said. "I didn't think minor-league ballplayers made much money, but maybe he's doing okay in the business world."

"Each of the three cases was thrown out because of a lack of evidence."

"And what were the charges for these cases?"

"Same thing each time. Sexual assault of a minor."

It felt like someone had swung a baseball bat into my chest. I took in a breath and shared a quick glance with Alex.

"Thanks for the info, Delmer," Alex said. "Nick, anything back from Agent Tanner?"

"Nothing. It's like the guy is on a four-hour lunch break."

Alex looked straight out the windshield, her face turning a hot pink. "Well, let us know if you learn anything else. We'll be in touch."

She ended the call and then checked her map application. "Ten miles until we reach The Wild Thing."

"So, to find out where Angel is, are you thinking we should sweet-talk old Travis, or threaten him within an inch of his life?"

Alex looked at me, her cheeks still pink. "A fastball straight at his head."

"Damn, I like the way your mind works."

Thirty-One

Alex

Our first trip to The Wild Thing told us two things: the parking lot was completely vacant, which made sense. It was too early for a bar to be open. Secondly, from the outside, it appeared to be a dump. There was graffiti on the sidewalk leading up to the front door, which was a checkerboard of wooden planks and foggy glass. The green paint job on the building looked like it had survived a tornado, and there were all sorts of debris in the parking lot.

Ivy and I located a burger joint and grabbed a bite to eat. Over burgers and Diet Cokes—we both liked the same unhealthy beverage—we shared our life stories with each other. It was kind of cool, opening up to a female friend. I had so many men in my life, I usually didn't have much of a chance to share my hopes and fears with other women.

I used to do that with Ezzy, but she was more like an elderly parent now, which was similar to having a young child, except more ornery. With Brad, I shared everything. He was a good listener and supported me through all the peaks and valleys that was my life. For a life partner, what else could a woman want?

But with a woman, it was different. Well, with Ivy it was

different. She was surprisingly open about the trauma she'd experienced as a kid growing up through the Texas foster care system. She also was very curious about my life, and I didn't hold back. Maybe it was because of almost losing Erin that I just didn't have the energy or desire to put up fences.

We both cleaned our plates. The waitress came by and picked up the dirty dishes. Ivy and I paused our conversation, both of us jiggling ice from our glasses into our mouths.

"I really don't know you very well," Ivy said, tossing her napkin on the table, "but for some reason, I just dumped all this stuff out there. Do you go through Jedi mind-trick class when you train to become an FBI agent?"

I snickered. "Hardly. I was interested, truly. Nick had told me a little about you. And I just knew, in the little we'd interacted over the phone, that we shared some things in common."

She nodded, crunched on another piece of ice. "You were pretty transparent yourself, Alex. You showed a lot of guts being able to move on after what happened to Mark. And then you found Brad...or he found you. But it works. For you, your family. It's pretty cool to hear. I've only loved one man, Saul. And it's because I was too afraid before that to cross the line and open up to someone."

I shrugged. "Or maybe it just took you a while to find the right person."

She chuckled. "Yeah, Saul is special. He has to be to put up with some of my bull-headedness."

"You too, huh?" I said with a smile.

We both nodded, staring at each other an extra second. Ivy had washed off her face, and she didn't appear to be wearing any makeup. She was just shy of my height of five-six and in good shape but probably not quite as toned as I was—I had to be, in my job. Her hair had some curls, some of which had been shocked into a frizz. She was a little closer to strawberry blonde than straight blonde like me.

I pushed a lock of hair out of my eyes and noticed she was staring at me again.

"What?"

"I don't know. Nothing, I guess."

"That means it's something. Do I have ketchup on my face?"

"No. Just noticing your features." She touched her nose and cheeks, and then her hair. "Something about you looks familiar. But I know we haven't met."

I bent my head forward and pointed at my scalp. "See that?"

"See what?" She giggled.

I lifted up. "Exactly. You see it. Gray is starting to creep in. It blends in pretty well with the blonde. Brad hasn't said a word, although I'm certain he's noticed."

She waved a hand in front of her face. "I rarely wear makeup or put on nice clothes. I'm surprised Saul will go out with me in public."

"But you have that natural beauty. My natural looks are being taken over by Mother Time."

"Fuck Father Time, right?"

I almost snorted out a laugh as I held up my cup. "Too bad we can't get a little whiskey with this Diet Coke. What a week it's been."

"If they had it, the whiskey would have to be…"

She was leading me, and I knew exactly where she was going. "Knob Creek," I said. "Sounds like you've had a drink with Mr. Tall, Blonde, and Handsome."

She nodded. "Mr. Ozzie Novak, of course. But you can't call him handsome. He's just…I don't know."

There were a few seconds of silence, and then I said, "Did you hear about Nicole and how he was framed for her murder?"

She set her cup down and clasped her hands. "Stan filled me in on everything. It was gut-wrenching to hear. Everything he's been through…and then to be framed by an old college friend." She sighed. I followed her gaze out the window as the sun dropped behind the hills.

She turned back to me. "But I also heard you guys took down the people who ran that terrorist organization."

"JustWin. Yep. Well, most of them. One got away. The one who killed Gretchen."

She let her arm drop to the table. "Gretchen? I didn't know. I'm so sorry."

I gave her an abbreviated summary of how Gretchen had been brainwashed by this agent of JustWin, leading her to turn on us, set up my boss, Jerry, and then turn a gun on me. "I'd convinced her to put the gun down. And that's when that JustWin agent killed her using some type of sniper rifle. Since then, it's been weird. And now Delmer is, more or less, part of the team."

I received a text from Brad saying he'd picked up Erin at the airport and was on his way back to the house. I sent a quick reply, thanking him. Ivy paid the bill and scooted out of the booth. We each put an arm around the other for a quick, bonding hug. It seemed so normal, as if we'd done it a million times.

She walked to the other side of the car and put a hand on the driver's-side door handle. "What's your take on Lady Di telling us about those Russians looking for that woman…uh, Olivia Bradshaw, if that's her actual name?"

"Meaning, do I think Lady Di was telling us the truth?"

She nodded.

"No reason for her to lie, I suppose." A highway-patrol car sped by with its red and blue lights flashing. I had an instant thought of Officer Bruce Massey. I wondered if he still had a job. I said to Ivy, "It does seem a little… I don't know, strange that these three Russians are looking for this woman at the same time we're looking for Angel."

Ivy tapped my shoulder. "You know what Ozzie would call that?"

I lifted my head. "A coincidence. Ozzie and I went to the same law school and were taught the same thing—that you can't build a case on a coincidence."

She tilted her head. "I hear ya. But we're not building a case. We're just trying to find a girl who's in danger. Let's go see if we can find her."

Thirty-Two

Ivy

By the time Alex and I reached The Wild Thing, we could see stars glowing against the endless nighttime sky. The parking lot was full, and the thud of music could be heard the moment I shut the car door. The song was some mash-up combination of rap and honky-tonk.

Alex put a hand to her ear. "Sounds like they're playing the classics at The Wild Thing. Classic *bullshit*."

"So, how are we going to play this?" I asked as we walked toward the building.

The front door to the bar slammed open, and a man stumbled out, dropped to his knees, and barfed near our feet. We jumped backward.

"Eeww!" I said, instantly feeling nauseated.

Alex scooted through the door. "I think we're going to have to wing it." I pulled up next to her and took in the scene. It looked like a room of modern-day pirates. Lots of do-rags, piercings on every visible body part, lots of skin showing on the few women in the place who weren't waitresses, and enough ink on said skin to make me think they had an onsite tattoo business. Was it legal to have a tattoo business in a drinking establishment?

This was Vegas, or close enough to it—there were no rules, apparently.

None of the waitresses looked our way, so we found the only two chairs that weren't taken. A minute later, a woman who was built like a bean-bag chair walked up and threw down two napkins. They didn't slide on the tabletop. They couldn't, because the table was coated with a sticky goo.

"Welcome to The Wild Thing. Would you like to try one of our homemade appetizers or craft beers?" She yawned in the middle of her pitch, which already had little enthusiasm.

"You have appetizers here?" I asked.

She shook her head out of a daze. "You actually want to try one?"

I gave her a half-shrug.

"If you're serious, I'm going to have to go find out if the microwave is actually working." She started to walk off,

"That's okay," Alex said. "We're not really hungry. How about your wine?"

"Okay, we've got two kinds. House red and house white. Well, now that I think about it, the last time I saw the bottle of red, there was something floating in it. So, I guess we just have the house white."

Alex said, "I'll take one of those."

"Just give me a beer. What do you have?" I asked, scanning the room.

The woman, whose complexion looked like that of a frog's, cringed. "I hope you weren't really counting on craft beers. Travis just makes us open a bottle in the back and then put it in a fancier glass."

"So, what kind of beer do you have?"

She held out a hand and tapped a finger. "Bud, Bud Light…" She paused, looked off for a second. "We're out of everything else."

"Bud Light it is."

She nodded, smiled. She was missing a front tooth. "I'll give you some pretzels since you're being so cool about everything."

"Thank you," Alex said. "What did you say your name was?"

"I didn't. It's Gertrude, but everyone calls me Gertie, ever since my days of working the shows on the strip." She nearly broke into a smile again, but it never quite got there. We were all distracted by a nearby table where two guys were ranting about being screwed over at some casino.

"You were a dancer?" I asked.

"I helped put on all the shows behind the scenes. 'Production assistant' was my formal title." She had sadness in her voice. "Back in a minute, ladies." She tapped the table and was off.

The two men at the table next to us were joined by two other men and a woman. The woman was moving from lap to lap in that slutty kind of way. Hired for the night, was my best guess.

Gertie returned with our drinks and a bowlful of pretzels. I sipped the beer and then chewed on a pretzel—it was stale. And the beer tasted…off. But was it the beer or my stomach? Normally, I had an iron stomach.

"Sorry if those pretzels aren't very fresh. This place is such a dump," she said, rolling her eyes. "I just wish I could make it back to the strip, like the good old days."

Alex drank a gulp of her wine. Her face looked like she'd just downed ten lemons. "So what's stopping you?" she asked.

Gertie turned and watched the people at the nearby table yelling at each other, the sole woman essentially doing lap dances for the men. Apparently, nothing was too shocking at The Wild Thing. She looked back at us. "I kind of screwed up a few years ago." Her chest lifted with a heavy sigh. "I got caught dealing dope to some of the showgirls. They had a no-tolerance policy, and I got black-listed. Just like that, I was on the outside looking in. Travis gave me a job. So, I do my thing, keep my mouth shut, and wait."

"Wait for what?" I asked.

"Time to pass, I guess. I just figured if enough time goes by, enough people will move on and I can go back to the glitz and glamour."

I gave her an encouraging nod. "Good for you, Gertie. I'm sure your patience will pay off." I didn't believe a word I was saying. "So, Travis is a pretty good boss?"

Something crossed her face, and it wasn't a positive expression. She tried to recover. "He pays me a fair wage, let's me keep all my tips, and doesn't let any of the men or women mess with me. So, I've got no real gripes." Her tone wasn't very convincing.

Alex looked at me, then turned to Gertie. "Hey, is this the place where the owner used to play baseball…some great pitcher, I think?"

"That's Travis," she said. "He's a little…uh, eccentric. But most of the time he tries to do the right thing."

Eccentric. Was that her way of justifying not saying anything about Travis's interactions with young girls? Then again, maybe he hid that part of his life from his bar employees. It would be the sensible thing to do.

"Well, you ladies just holler if you need anything," Gertie said, tapping the table twice. "This place is a little on the rough side. And I can tell you're much better tippers than the rest of these ass-clowns." She went still. Her eyes looked over my shoulder. I wanted to turn around, but something told me I shouldn't. A few seconds later, three men walked by. They all wore hats and leather jackets and had the same barrel-chested physiques and patch of hair on their chins. They slipped behind a curtain in the back.

Gertie exhaled, but her breathing came out in short bursts.

"What's wrong, Gertie?" Alex asked.

"Nothing," she said all too quickly. Her eyes didn't settle on anything for a few seconds. She looked like she'd been hit on the head with a frying pan.

"If there's something wrong, Gertie, you can talk to us," I said. "We're just a couple of gals who are driving through Nevada on our way to LA. My friend, Alex, has friends in the movie business."

She smiled, but it was as though her foundation had been altered.

"Are you afraid, Gertie?" Alex asked.

"I can't talk about anything. Not now." She looked at each of us pointedly—she had a story to tell—but she quickly turned away, walked over to another table, and picked up empty beer bottles.

Alex and I gave each other a knowing glance. I leaned in closer to her. "You think they're the three Russians that Lady Di talked about earlier?"

"Maybe."

"But will it help us find Angel?"

"Well, we either ask them—which might mean we end up confronting Travis at the same time—or corner Gertie. And right now, since I'm not carrying, I don't like our odds against the three Russian tanks and this Wild guy."

We paid our bill, tipping Gertie quite nicely, and then left the building.

Thirty-Three

Alex

Ivy drove us to the side of the building—where we could see both the front and back doors—and we waited for Gertie to leave. Over the next three hours, the bar slowly emptied of the riffraff and two other waitresses. With only a handful of cars left in the lot, we finally saw her exit the back door. I quickly got out of the car and met her at her old Toyota before she opened the door. Ivy pulled up next to us.

"Dear God, you scared me to death," she said, a hand to her chest. She looked at me, then at Ivy. "Why are you trolling me? I thought you were nice, normal…something we don't usually see at the bar. Are you just trying to scam me or something? If you are, I don't have any money on me."

"It's nothing like that, Gertie," Ivy said. "We want to help you."

"Help?" She chuckled. "How can you help me?" She snapped her fingers, then pointed at me. "Wait, you're the one with the Hollywood connections. You think you can get me a job in LA? Now, that would be the greatest miracle. Putting Vegas in the rearview mirror."

Damn, I wished Ivy hadn't gone there. "I don't know, Gertie.

I'll have to talk to some people. We can see you're a good person, though. Someone who tries to do the right thing."

She gave a slow nod, as if she wanted to believe it but wasn't sure.

I opened the picture of Angel on my phone and showed it to Gertie. While there was a single yellow light attached to the side of the building, the glow of my phone lit up Gertie's face.

"Never seen her," she said.

"Are you sure?" Ivy pulled my hand closer to Gertie's eyes.

"I'm pretty good with faces, and…well, she's not been here. I mean, I don't recognize her."

I traded a quick glance with Ivy. "Gertie, we need to find her. She's in danger. Her mother sold her to a drug dealer for drugs. And we think—"

"Travis." She sounded as though someone had punched her in the gut.

"So, you know about what he does with young girls?"

She brought a hand to her face. "I didn't want to believe it. I try to keep to myself. Everyone does at The Wild Thing. Mostly."

There was something else there. But we had to keep the focus on Angel. "Gertie, what have you seen?" Ivy asked.

Her eyes became glassy. "Things." She shook her head and swallowed. "Stop it, Gertie. Stop ignoring everything." She was talking to herself. She licked her lips and looked at me. "A few times over the last few months, I've seen a few girls up here."

"And what happened to them?" Ivy asked.

She shrugged. "I don't really know. Although there was one time when I saw one of them put into a fancy sedan, and the car drove off. Never saw her again after that."

"Gertie, we need to better understand what Travis does in his side businesses."

"Oh, you hit the nail on the head there. He's got all sorts of shit on the side."

"Who with? What kind of details can you give us?" Ivy rattled off.

She flinched a bit, took a step back, and gave us both the once-over. "Who are you two with? The cops?"

Tim to come clean. "Gertie, I work for the FBI."

"And I work for Angel's father," Ivy said. "He's heartbroken over what his wife did—trading their daughter to pay off a drug debt."

"What kind of drugs?" she asked.

"Fentanyl. It's a type of—"

"I know, I know. It's an opioid. It's all the rage in these parts."

"And is that one of Travis's side businesses?"

She nodded like a little girl. "I've seen open boxes with pills. I never tried the shit. But I know people who have, and they've never been the same. Two of my friends have died from it."

And she'd never done or said anything? She was, essentially, complicit in some of these crimes. I withheld my anger, knowing things weren't always black-and-white.

"I'm sorry about your friends, Gertie. But it's not too late to do something about all this. The drug business, the girls… We need to stop it."

"Dmitri," she said.

"Who's that?" I asked.

"He's this Russian cat that comes in and meets with Travis. I've heard them talking."

"About?"

"Trading girls for the drugs. They use the street terms, like murder eight, tango and cash, China girl."

My mind swam with ideas on where this could go. But the main person who came to mind was the man with the thick accent who wore the Carter mask. "Does Dmitri wear nice clothes and look like he's just had a manicure?"

"Good-looking guy, yeah. And he likes the finer things—that's pretty obvious. I saw him get into a Jag one time. He's the exact opposite of Travis. Travis is smarter than he looks, but he's white trash in my books."

And yet she'd still said nothing. I took in a deep breath, but Ivy beat me to it.

"Gertie, we think Travis could have Angel. Or maybe he did something with her."

"Like trade her to Dmitri?" Gertie asked hesitantly.

"Do you know if Travis did that?"

"Like I said, *I* haven't seen Angel."

"But..." I gestured with my hand for her to continue. She did.

"It's all so fucked up now. Dammit!"

"What is it, Gertie?"

She released a heavy breath. "Liv...I knew she was curious about what Travis and Dmitri were up to. I just tried to stay out of it."

Right, like bury your head in the sand. But that name—Liv—was one of the names Lady Di had thrown out there. The three Russians had asked about her.

"Earlier in the bar, Gertie, three men walked in, and I saw something about you change. You were scared. Why?"

Her eyes were wide with fear again. "I think they're looking for Liv."

"So Liv works at The Wild Thing?"

"Until she disappeared a couple of days ago."

"Someone took her? Or she just vanished?"

"I'm not completely sure." A tear rolled down her cheek.

"Why would someone take her?" Ivy asked.

I spoke before Gertie could respond. "Or why would she have a need to vanish?"

"I don't know the answer to either question. She's a nice person...kind of a friend to me, although she kept her distance. Never wanted to hang out or do anything."

"There's got to be something else here, Gertie. Did you see something that maybe you forgot to tell us?"

She wiped her face. She looked like she'd aged five years in the few minutes we'd spoken. Her face had red splotches, and shadows made her wrinkles more prominent. She looked down and kicked some rocks.

"Gertie?"

She lifted her head and blinked hard. "Liv seemed to be curious about a couple of the girls that Travis brought in the back. I turned a blind eye—I was selfish and afraid. But she couldn't help herself. I warned her not to get too close. But I wonder if she did."

"Too close to...?"

"Meddling in Travis's business? Maybe to one of the girls? I don't know what she did."

Ivy turned to me. "Could she have Angel?"

"It's possible, I suppose." I looked at Gertie, who was about to speak when a door opened behind us. I glanced over my shoulder and saw the three Russian tanks from earlier. Two were speaking in their native tongue, but the one in front eyed us as they walked to a blue minivan and got in.

"Here's the crazy thing," Gertie said under her breath, even though the guys were in a car at least a hundred feet from us. "Those three Russians are the Bar Act at Circus Circus."

"A drinking bar?" Ivy asked.

The blue minivan drove out of our sight, around the building.

"No, it's an act where two guys hold up either end of the bar, and the person on top of the bar does all sorts of flips and twists. They actually call themselves "The Three Amigos"—that's a running joke."

Interesting tidbit, certainly, but was it relevant? Probably not. I touched Ivy's elbow. "I wonder if they're connected to Dmitri."

Gertie jumped in. "I don't know how, and I can't prove it, but I think they are."

I looked at Ivy. "So, why would Dmitri—he's Carter from my earlier experience—want to find Liv?"

Ivy shook her head. "I wish we could ask her. Maybe she knows something about Angel and got scared off. Who knows? She could be across the country by now."

I tapped a finger to my chin. "What if Liv somehow grabbed Angel before Travis did something with her, and so the Russians say they're looking for Liv, but they're really looking for Angel?"

Ivy shrugged. "I guess it's possible. It's certainly a theory."

"One we can't prove, though."

"I wish I could do more," Gertie said, thumbing another tear in the corner of her eye. "I just wish I'd said something before now."

"Better now than never," Ivy said.

The blue minivan skidded to a stop next to us, and the door flew open. The Russians. The one with a red cap jumped out and aimed a pistol right at me.

"Get in van," he said in broken English. I saw one of his comrades in the van also holding a gun.

We paused a second. My heart was peppering my chest like a drum.

A gasp from behind me. "Dear God, we're going to die," Gertie said.

I had to bring calm to the scene. "Let's just get in the…"

The man extended his gun and fired the weapon. The sound—only a couple of feet from my ear—jolted me.

"No!" Ivy cried out.

I turned and saw Gertie's body flopping to the ground.

"Get in van. Now!" Red Cap said.

Ivy reached down for Gertie—she brought a hand to her mouth. "I might vomit."

There was nothing left of Gertie's face.

More yelling at us, mostly in Russian, from inside the van. With no other options, Ivy and I complied and got into the van.

Thirty-Four

Ivy

I sat in the back seat with one of the gunmen—he wore no hat, showing off his chrome dome—and Alex sat in the middle seat next to the other one holding a gun. The driver wore a black cap and was on his phone speaking in Russian as we rolled out of the parking lot and onto the highway.

A phone was shoved in my face by Chrome. "You know her?" His pistol was still aimed at my side. I looked at the photo on the phone. It was a woman with short, black hair and lots of piercings and tats. She looked like the typical clientele at The Wild Thing.

"Never seen her before," I said, shaking my head.

He turned the phone to Alex, who was sitting directly in front of me. "You…you know her?"

She held her gaze an extra beat. "Nope."

The three of them started yelling at each other in Russian, even as the driver stayed on his cell-phone call. They were under pressure, it seemed, to find this Liv person and bring her somewhere. She had to be incredibly important to them, but I had no idea why. Maybe Liv had been caught up in the drug web, similar to Alex. My thoughts took another leap: if Dmitri—the person Alex believed was the fake Jimmy Carter—was behind all this, then he probably would like nothing better than to have Alex brought to him. Did he even know The Three Amigos had Alex—his former drug runner—in the van?

I only wanted to learn where Angel was. And with Travis likely being back at the bar, I feared that we'd lost our chance at finding her. Hell, we might be her only chance to not be sold into prostitution, or to avoid death. And look at us. We might not even live to see the next sunrise.

Out of nowhere, images of Saul's syrupy eyes and brilliant smile popped into my mind. His smile was always the brightest when we were tickling each other, or teasing the other one for some reason. We'd grown so close over the last year. He'd been the man who'd finally melted the walls I'd erected since my earliest childhood memories. I'd been with a few other men, but they never really respected me, probably because I hadn't really respected myself. For years, I'd blamed myself, at least partially, for all the sick and perverted acts of adults—people who were supposed to care for me, if not love me.

Saul, though, didn't try to change me. He simply accepted me. He embraced our friendship, and, over time, our passion surged into a stratosphere I'd never thought possible. Not for me. So many memories from our Caribbean cruise, some adventurous, some just flat-out fun—like zip-lining through a rain forest—some that made my heart skip a beat for the right reasons. I loved that man. I had a future with the man. My other passion—to save kids from the horrors of abuse—had, once again, blinded me to danger. Saul had warned me, but he didn't stop me. He knew I'd resent him if he pushed too hard.

Damn, I wished I'd listened. A future of happiness and true love and even a family—something I thought was only good enough for *other people*—was to be my destiny with Saul. Until now. Maybe fate had a different idea of how my life would play out. The ending looked frighteningly close.

But what about Angel? That poor girl had been sold by her own mother. Some perverted heathen most likely had her—whether that was Travis Wild or some other twisted fuck. Could she have escaped with this Liv person? Oh, how I wished. If so, I hoped that woman was far away from this place, maybe in some law-enforcement office, or on her way back to San Antonio to find Angel's father.

As The Three Amigos continued their yelling match, I caught Alex's wandering eye. This was not the eye of someone who had resigned herself to death, or at least to the fact that we could do nothing more than hope they released us. She had that look of determination…of defiance.

I immediately felt emboldened by her lack of fear, by doing whatever it took to survive. Without moving her head, I saw her eyes dart to Chrome, then over to Red, and then up to the driver. She did this several times. She had a plan of some kind. At least I thought she did. I couldn't imagine how it wouldn't result in one or both of us being injured or killed, but she was the expert at this stuff.

I only wondered how long she'd wait. We were on a flat, black stretch of highway. A small, dark building was coming up on our left. I tried to think of scenarios that might give us an advantage. Outside of passing some topless showgirls who might distract our kidnappers—in the middle of nowhere—I couldn't imagine what Alex was looking for. Maybe she would deem the risk too great. Maybe she'd wait until we reached our destination and then reassess our odds there.

Maybe she'd only wait five seconds.

Actually, it was more like four seconds when Alex gave a straight-line jab with her knuckles directly into the throat of Red.

His eyes bulged, and he gurgled like he'd swallowed his tongue. She reached over, grabbed his gun hand, and fired the pistol into his knee.

Damn.

Red screamed as Chrome lifted his gun toward Alex. I swung my elbow into his arm just as the gun fired—the bullet ricocheted off the roof. The minivan swerved left and right. Chrome threw a punch at my face. Somehow, I dodged it. Copying Alex, I threw a jab into his throat. Similar results. I would have smiled had we not been fighting for our lives. He let go of the gun.

I grabbed it as Alex snatched the gun from Red and whipped the butt of the gun off the head of the driver. He cried out. The minivan swung violently—we went up on two wheels. Everyone who could breathe was yelling. We teetered for another second, and then the van crashed onto its side. Glass sprayed everywhere. Without a seatbelt on, I was tossed around like a coin in a tin can. The minivan rammed into a boulder, which sent me tumbling through the cabin.

A moment of silence. A breath. I touched my head and felt blood. Then I heard some moans.

"Quick, Ivy, get out of the car." Alex pushed herself upward through the partially open sliding door.

I looked up and saw stars in the sky, and I moved toward those stars through the hole. As I pulled my legs up, one of the men grabbed my ankle.

"Let go!" I kicked at him, but his grip was solid. "Alex, where's the gun?"

"I lost it in the crash."

I'd lost the gun I'd picked up as well.

She moved to her feet, hooked her arms under my armpits, and pulled until she screamed. It wasn't helping—I felt like I was being yanked out of my own skin.

Then I heard a chuckle—a deprived chuckle. I went spastic. Alex backed up a step. I flailed my whole body, torquing it without any pattern. The Russian's hand finally let go, and I quickly pulled my leg upward. Alex and I climbed off the minivan. The headlights were still on, and the wheels were still spinning. Smoke billowed out of the crushed front hood. Glass crunched under our shoes.

We came around to the front of the minivan. That was when I saw the arm reaching out of the cracked opening of the windshield. "Gun!" I yelled.

Alex, moving like a panther, swung her foot like a punter and connected with the hand. The gun flew onto the ground. She ran over and grabbed it just as the man was exiting the minivan. He rushed at her—she fired the gun at his chest. He stumbled forward and dropped at her feet.

Cool as a cucumber, she said, "Need to see if the other two are conscious."

We looked inside the van. The other two were either dead or close to it. Their eyes were closed, and there was a lot of blood.

"What now?" I said, breathing like I'd run a marathon.

I could see cuts up and down her arms and on her neck. "You need medical attention," I said.

"Same for you," she replied. Then she turned and faced the back of the building. It looked like an old gas station that hadn't been used in years.

"We might be able to find a car we can use here," she said, moving over to a car bay that was covered by a vertical sliding door.

She'd obviously hit her head during the crash. This place looked like it hadn't been open since Eisenhower was in office. "Wait, is this the place you mentioned in your story?"

"Yep."

We quickly looked for a way inside and found none. The darkness of the night didn't help. But with the aid of the headlights from the crashed minivan on the backside of the building, we spotted a padlock on the bay door. Alex fired the pistol into the lock—it exploded into tiny pieces. She pulled a chain, and the door opened.

"No car," she said, dejectedly. "We might need to walk all the way back to The Wild Thing. Or flag down a car on the highway."

I blew out a breath and walked into the darkened space.

That's when I heard the whimpering of a girl.

Thirty-Five

Alex

"Did you hear that?" Ivy asked me.

"Hear what?"

Ivy had disappeared into the black abyss of the garage. "Watch out," I said. "They might have traps set up or something crazy."

She didn't reply.

"Ivy, what are you doing?"

A moment later, she came out of the darkness, holding the hand of a girl with tight curls. I couldn't believe my eyes.

"Angel?"

She sniffled, her eyes squinting from the headlights of the minivan. "Yes, it's me."

"She was curled up in the corner, eating a package of cheese and crackers," Ivy said.

"How did you escape? How long have you been in there? Are you okay?"

Ivy held up a hand. She was right. I needed to hold off on my inquisition for the moment.

"She had help," Ivy said, motioning over her shoulder. All I saw was darkness.

"I wouldn't be alive if it wasn't for her," Angel said, looking into the dark garage. "Or I'd be some sex slave to a Montana rancher. God sent an angel to Angel." She giggled through her tears.

I wasn't quite getting it, although the emotion in our space was intense.

"Liv, it's okay," Angel called out. "Ivy was sent here by my dad. Alex is an FBI agent who knows Ivy. We can trust 'em."

A figure emerged from the garage. It was the same person from the photo the Russian had shown me. She walked closer, and I could see the piercings in her eyebrows and nose and many in her ears. A snake tattoo wrapped around her neck. She had short, black hair.

"Hi, Alex," she said.

I knew that voice. I knew those eyes—a honey brown. And I *knew her*. I blinked a few times to make sure I wasn't imagining it.

"Liv has been the best," Angel said. "That crazy man, Travis, was about to sell me like a head of cattle to some rancher living in Montana. But they started arguing over the price, and that's when Liv walked into the back room, grabbed me, and ran out the front door. We've been on the run, hiding ever since."

Liv's eyes went to her, then back to me.

Ivy walked over and put a hand on my shoulder. We locked eyes for a second. We both knew who this was, but we couldn't say anything. Not now, not in front of Angel.

I turned back to the biker-looking woman. "Is that true…Liv?"

"Yes."

I had a hundred questions for her, but I couldn't ask them. I couldn't stop staring at her. Ivy nudged me. "Cops or someone might drive by and see this…mess."

"They can't find me. I don't trust them," Liv said, backpedaling.

"It will be okay." I touched my back pocket. My phone was gone. Probably destroyed in the crash. I brushed some loose hair out of my face and looked at Ivy. "I'm not sure I want all of us walking back to the Wild Thing to get your car. Too risky. I can go."

"But what if something happens to you? It's too risky to go alone. We need to stick together and get to someone we trust."

I knew all it would take was a call to Jerry, and then we'd have to wait a few hours. I looked down at the gun I was holding. If I had to guess, I'd say it was a Russian-made Makarov, a .38. I tucked it into the back of my pants. "I'm going to flag down a car. You guys have to trust me that this will work. I don't want you freaking out when I get someone to pull over and take us in."

Angel nodded.

Ivy said, "You know I'm with you, Alex. But what if you flag down the wrong person?"

"I have to believe there are more good people in this God-forsaken place than bad."

I then looked at Liv.

"Trust isn't a word I use very much." She took in a shallow breath.

My eyes went to that sick snake tattoo and then her shoulders and arms. She was cut like a wrestler. Oh, so many questions. But I also could sense that the answers were complex and cloaked in secrecy and fear. We'd have time for that later. I hoped so anyway.

I told everyone to huddle together on the side of the building. I walked to the edge of the highway, and within a couple of minutes, I saw the headlights of a car. I moved closer to the edge of the pavement, and as the car closed to within a hundred yards,

I started waving my arms. The car—it looked like Ferrari of some kind—zipped by without even slowing down. Probably for the better, since I knew we couldn't fit the four of us in that vehicle. It was almost impossible to see what kind of car was approaching in the dark of the night.

Another pair of headlights snagged my attention. These were higher off the road than that of the Ferrari. I knew I couldn't waste time, but I also knew that if the wrong person was driving this vehicle, we could all end up dead, or at least captured. I glanced to the side of the building. I could see the three of them huddled together. Back to the road. The vehicle was fast approaching. I didn't have the luxury of putting every driver through a screening process. I only saw one choice.

I moved out into the middle of the lane and waved my arms. The driver veered across the yellow line. He or she was trying to get around me. "Fucker!" I yelled, shifting to my right.

"What are you doing, Alex? You're going to get yourself killed."

That was Ivy. I ignored her and held my ground. A second later, the vehicle veered right. I was pretty sure it was an SUV. Without thinking, I pulled out my pistol, lowered my stance, and aimed it right at the windshield, toward the driver's side.

The driver hit the brakes. The SUV vibrated violently and came to a stop two feet in front of me. I walked over to the driver's side, and the window slid down. I could hear a woman yelling from inside, but the driver was a man…with big ears.

"What the hell, lady?" he asked as I walked up, the gun at my side.

It was Officer Bruce Massey—the guy whom I'd dropped in the middle of nowhere with no clothes. His eyes locked on mine. I didn't immediately respond.

"Bruce, baby, is she going to hurt us?"

I looked beyond Bruce and saw a woman who was reaching toward the back, where there was a baby in a car seat.

"Me and my friends just need a ride."

He clenched his jaw, his eyes like saucers. He got out of the car and stood up.

"What are you doing, Bruce?"

"It's going to be okay, dear," he said to his wife while staring at me. Then, he seemed to notice the blood on my arms and neck. "You're injured."

"Long story. But my friends and I need some help."

"We were just on our way to my wife's parent's house. They live only about thirty minutes down the road on a ranch."

Perfect. "Can we tag along? I promise I'll make it worth your while."

He cocked his head back, then muttered, "My wife and child are in the car, and you're propositioning me?"

"No, not that. I work for the FBI."

"Right. And I'm a showgirl who works at a casino."

He didn't believe me. I got it.

"Bruce, I know you have some doubt, but—"

"I'd say it's a bit more than doubt. I almost lost everything that night…my job, my life, my family. It completely changed my outlook on the future and what I was doing with it."

"Great, Bruce. I'm happy for you. I really am. But we're in the middle of a critical situation. We could all end up dead if you don't help us…and that includes a fifteen-year-old girl who had been kidnapped until one of us rescued her. We're desperate. All we need is to make a phone call and then lie low for a few hours. The Bureau will do something to accommodate you for your help."

He turned his head, as if something had caught his eye. Something from behind the building?

"My friend and I were kidnapped from a parking lot of a bar using this gun. It's Russian. We crashed, and that's why I'm all cut up. At least one of them is dead. The other two, I'm not sure. They might be part of some Russian crime outfit. I don't know. But there are more of them."

"Okay, I'll call the cops for you." He started to turn around.

I reached out and grabbed his arm. "Can't do that. They might be in the back pocket of Cadillac."

"Travis Wild?"

"So you know about him?"

"I've heard…stories," he said, moving his head left and then right.

He looked back into the car, then turned and scratched the back of his head. "Okay. Get your friends in the back. I'll talk to my wife. Your bosses at the FBI are going to have to be very convincing."

"They will be. Don't worry."

I whistled for the others, and we jumped into the SUV. We were safe. For now.

Thirty-Six

Alex

Just as I'd hoped, it took only one phone call. Jerry listened intently for ten minutes, and then he told me he was calling Assistant Director Barry Holt—the same man who'd once thought Jerry had committed treason and was behind a series of bombings. Of course, we learned that he'd been set up. Jerry didn't hold any long-term grudges against Holt, at least nothing that would stop him from making the right decision. And he said calling Holt was the right decision. He told me to hold tight for an hour and he'd get back to me with a plan.

It took him only thirty minutes. I hung up the phone and saw Ivy standing at the doorway of the screened-in porch.

"Where's Angel?" I asked.

Ivy walked in as some bug chirped and hissed in the darkness behind the house. I stole a glance over my shoulder. I could feel something spindly crawling up my spine. For a moment, I wondered if Dmitri or Travis, or both of them, had somehow found out we were at the Massey Ranch—I'd seen a stone sign by the front gate—and were about to light the place up with gunfire.

"Did you hear me? I said Angel is tied at the hip with,

uh…Liv," Ivy said.

"Sorry. Just thinking."

"Whew. For a moment there, I thought you had lost your hearing, like Ozzie."

We held our gaze for an extra beat. "Ozzie," I said, nodding. "I'm not sure what to do or where to begin with my questions for—"

"Hey, ladies."

It was Bruce, who'd stuck his head into our space.

"Hey, Bruce. What's going on?"

"Did you make your call?"

I saw a clocked perched above the doorway. It was just after midnight. "You can tell your wife and in-laws that our ticket out of here should arrive within seven hours. Maybe sooner."

"Good." He walked over to Ivy and me. "Because," he said in a muted tone, "I hate lying to them."

I cocked my head—what was his point?

"I told you, Alex, that I've changed. And one of the things I told myself was that I wouldn't lie to my wife ever again."

I wanted to mock his lack of sincerity. But he sounded like a changed man, and for that, I felt guilty and happy for him at the same time. "Sorry we're putting you and your family through this ordeal."

"It's not like I really had a choice. You had a gun, and you had information that would have ruined my life. So…" He stuffed his hands into his jeans pockets and looked off for a moment. He had this pouting look. A picture formed of what Bruce with the big ears looked like as a little kid.

I said, "For what it's worth, I would have never used the gun."

Ivy snorted out a laugh. A few seconds passed, and then Bruce's lips finally turned up at the edges. "Funny, funny, ha-ha."

The joke's on Bruce," he said, rolling his eyes.

"By the way, what story did you tell your in-laws?"

He twisted his lips, shuffled his feet.

"I really don't care what you told them as long as they don't call anyone and tell them we're here. I don't know who they know. From what I've heard, the people we're dealing with are very connected…and protected by the establishment."

"No worries on that front," he said. "My in-laws have a marijuana farm out back. They're good people, but they're also entrepreneurs. So, they keep a low profile, if you know what I mean. They don't talk about their side business, though, not even to my wife and me."

"What did you tell them about us?" Ivy asked.

"You're going to laugh."

"Try me," I said.

"I said you were the daughter of a US senator from Texas and that you'd escaped from a state hospital."

"You told them I was a looney?"

He nodded, though winced slightly, as if I might slap him.

"I'm fine with that. But what about everyone else—Ivy, Angel, and, uh…?"

"Liv. I just said you picked up this vagabond group on your trip across the country. Anyway, I told them it would only take until daybreak before I could get someone from a local hospital to come pick you up. And then I'd help the others find their way back to whatever home they came from."

"See? You're going to come across as very noble when this is over," I said.

"Only if I keep up the lie. And that will be exposed when your FBI buddies show up, right?"

"Good point."

He turned his palms to the ceiling. "So, like I said, I'm

hoping that between you and your bosses, you guys can help me out, so I don't have to explain how we *really* know each other."

"We'll think of something that will make you look good. Don't worry."

I could hear a baby crying in the distance.

"Gotta run. Family first," he said, holding up a finger.

Bruce ran off. Before Ivy and I could speak further, Angel and Liv joined us on the porch. We munched on a few salty snacks that Bruce had brought us and drank bottles of Bai, a tasty, fruity drink. We talked some and rested some. A few times, I noticed Liv looking at me. It seemed like she had this urge to open up to me—I certainly had a longing to ask her a million questions. But I also saw a sadness in her eyes. I couldn't understand her despondency, but I also hadn't heard her story. I just knew she didn't feel safe uttering a word with any other person around.

I got up and paced, occasionally glancing at the still area behind the home. Again, I asked myself if there was any way Dmitri, Travis, and their presidential goon squad were about to launch an attack. But did they actually want all of us dead? Or were they more interested in the value of Angel and Liv?

A few more hours passed, and no one attacked the ranch. Jerry, Holt, and a horde of agents arrived. The first order of business was explaining to Bruce's family why six dark SUVs pulled up in front of their house. I took Jerry and Holt to the side.

"Are these agents from the Vegas office?" I asked. "Because I know one agent who seemed like he's mailed it in."

"This office has been on our red-team list for some time. So, Tanner, the agent you're referring to, I believe, and a number of others will be brought in and charged this morning. Another team is handling that. This team with us, they've been handpicked."

"Good," I said, releasing a deep breath. I then explained to them what needed to happen before we left the ranch. Holt told Jerry to speak to Bruce's wife and in-laws—he said he'd tell them that Bruce was a hero and would be awarded an FBI medal for keeping these important people alive until the agents showed up.

Holt then asked me to follow him to speak to the others. The three young ladies were sitting on the porch. I introduced the assistant director.

"So, you're, like, really important. You get to talk to the president?" Angel asked, clearly in awe of his position.

"Sometimes. It's not very glamorous, I assure you, Angel."

He then told Angel that she, Ivy, and an agent would soon be leaving for San Antonio where she would be reunited with her family. Angel was so happy that she hugged the assistant director. He seemed a little uncomfortable, but he didn't fight it. Which was good. Angel needed to be able to trust that more people in this world had her back. Every kid needed that, regardless of their age.

The female agent who was going to accompany Angel and Ivy walked into the porch area. She and Angel started talking, and they walked out of our space, leaving Ivy and me there with Holt and Liv. They stared at each other for longer than normal. Something wasn't right. It was as though Holt knew Liv, which, based upon the pieces I'd put together, made sense. But he seemed hesitant, nervous even, in sharing information with her.

He rubbed his palms on his thighs and then asked her to take a seat. He proceeded to tell her a piece of news that made my knees buckle. She cried for a minute, but then she said she wasn't surprised. When she calmed, he said, "So, as a result of what I just shared, after we pick up Wild and Dmitri, there's no reason you can't resume your old life. That is, if you want it. If not, we'll place you somewhere else and let you start all over again.

It's your choice."

Then she unloaded everything that she'd experienced in the last few days to Ivy and me. By the time she finished, we were all in tears. Everyone except Holt, who checked his watch more than once. We three ladies then decided on the next steps.

Holt said, "We're headed out to Dmitri's new compound. We think Wild is onsite as well."

"You're not leaving without me," I said.

He held up a finger.

"I'm going, so don't fight me on this…sir."

He shrugged, extended a hand to the doorway.

It was time to catch some snakes, both Russian and American.

Thirty-Seven

Alex

The sex-drug trafficking compound in the rocky hills was near the border of Lincoln County. Wearing bullet-resistant vests and armed with submachine guns, thirty agents raided the two-story building that looked more like a prison. I saw iron bars on the windows and doors.

By the time I made it inside, agents had seven men lying face down on the floor with their hands cuffed behind their backs. I heard someone call for an ambulance—one of the girls was unconscious, apparently from taking one too many pills. A line of "customers" was escorted outside, where they were being questioned by a set of agents. I stayed inside until I could figure out which one was Dmitri. When I pointed him out—I could tell by his upscale attire—Jerry singlehandedly picked him up, dragged him into the kitchen, and threw him into a chair.

"Alex Troutt, how nice of you to join your little FBI raid."

I could see his smug face for the first time. His light-brown hair was parted on one side. He had a two-day beard, as if he were going for that rugged look. But I could tell he'd never really worked a day in his life—with his coifed attire and hoity-toity cologne and manicured nails and buttery smooth skin. It was all of those things, but mostly his smug look that told me he actually thought he was a different, better species than the rest of us. I could feel my insides harden into a pit.

"Jerry, leave us alone for a minute."

Jerry ran his fingers through his thinning hair. "No can do. You know that. Let me just take him away."

"It doesn't really matter what you do," Dmitri spat. "My embassy will have me out of your American jail in a matter of hours." He tried to move his arms, but he couldn't. "Diplomatic immunity, you know," he said with a smile, his teeth looking like they'd been painted white.

I guessed this maggot was connected to the official Russian ambassador's contingent.

"I wouldn't be so sure about your claim about diplomatic immunity," Jerry said. "Our lawyers might take a very different viewpoint."

Dmitri looked at Jerry as though he had no clue what he was talking about.

"I just want to know one thing, Carter," I said.

He winked. "I knew you liked that presidential theme."

I just stared at him and somehow withheld the urge to strangle him.

"Okay, you can stop with the devil eyes now, Alex Troutt. Ask your question or return me to the other room. You are…what Americans would say…creeping me out."

I lowered my body until we were eye to eye. "How did you know that by kidnapping my daughter you would have access to a mother who would have the skills to survive that drug run?" I despised this man.

He chuckled. "Maybe I'll tell you. Maybe I'll just let you wonder."

I asked Jerry to shut the kitchen door. As he walked over, I took a step back and then hurled a fist into Dmitri's face. He cried out as blood spewed.

"Oh crap, Alex," Jerry said, getting in between us.

"Get out of my way, Jerry."

"Can't."

"Jerry…"

"No more punching." He moved to the side.

"You going to tell me?" I asked Dmitri.

"Screw. You," he said.

I moved around Jerry, grabbed Dmitri's nose, and twisted like it was the handle of a wine-bottle opener. He squealed even more. "Okay, okay, okay. Stop, please!"

I did, and then he told me what I wanted to know.

I washed my hands at the sink and walked out of the kitchen. On the way through the living room, I saw Wild sitting up against the wall, handcuffed. No one was paying him much attention, so I kicked him in the face, then leaned down and said, "You will rot in hell for what you've done."

That created a stir. But I was done with them. I walked out the door.

Before I left Vegas, though, I had one more piece of unfinished business. Jerry said he'd tag along and provide moral support. I think it was because he wanted to make sure I didn't commit another felony.

Honestly, I wasn't entirely certain that I wouldn't.

Thirty-Eight

Alex

Jerry and I found the Faulks at poolside. Not surprisingly, Byron wore dark sunglasses and had a Bloody Mary in his hand.

Irony? I think not.

The sun reflected off the stone to radiate some serious heat. In the few seconds it took for us to walk about fifty feet, Jerry was wiping sweat from his pink face. I saw Becca and Sonya in the pool, tossing a ball back and forth, dodging a swarm of other swimmers. They didn't notice us as we pulled up next to Byron's lounge chair. Jerry's large body cast a shadow over Byron, who'd moved the straw to the side and was chugging his Blood Mary as if he'd been withheld any liquid substance for a week.

Jerry cleared his throat. Byron held up a finger, downing the last drop, then let out an "Ah" and wiped his mouth with his bare arm. He had on shorts and a short-sleeve T-shirt that highlighted the much-hyped Mayweather-McGregor fight in Vegas a while back. The fight, from what I recalled, had been mostly a farce. Just like Byron.

"Byron," I said.

He finally looked up. "Alex?" He lowered his sunglasses, shot a glance at Jerry. "What are you doing back in Vegas? And who's your, uh…friend?"

"Let's go inside and talk," I said, motioning toward the building with my head.

He splayed his arms. "This weather is beautiful. Why would I want to go inside?"

"I think we need to have a conversation, preferably away from the girls." I saw Sonya and Becca diving for the ball, giggling with each other. They seemed so happy. I wondered how many moments during a regular day in the Faulks' home they were allowed such a luxury. They still hadn't looked in our direction.

Byron lowered his glasses again, eyeing Jerry and me. "You never told me what you're doing back in Vegas, or who this guy is." He had a bit of a shaky-voice going on. I wasn't sure if it was because he was plastered…or if he had the sense that his past mistakes would no longer be cloaked in secrecy or brushed off as a typical problem of a suburban dad with a mortgage, and a wife and child, and pressures at work, and all the other responsibilities that came with his life.

"I'm here to talk to you, Byron. To give you the opportunity to answer a couple of important questions."

He grabbed his glass and tipped his head back. Nothing was in the glass except red-colored ice. He held up his empty. "Where's a damn waiter when you need one?"

"You don't need another drink. But you're probably going to need a lawyer," Jerry said.

Byron threw off his glasses, giving Jerry the once-over. "And who the hell are you?"

Jerry pulled out his credentials and extended his arm without saying a word.

"Of course, I don't have my FBI credentials," I said. "They were stolen, along with everything else. Including my daughter."

On the last three words, I could feel my own voice quivering. I took in a slow breath.

"I know you're upset, Alex. Sonya and I didn't sleep a wink until we got Becca back—thanks to you, I might add. But you should be happy now, back at home and enjoying your daughter. What in the world are you doing here with this guy?"

"He's my boss. He's my friend. Are you familiar with the term 'friend'?"

He tried to laugh, but he never got there. "Funny, Alex."

"I'm not fucking laughing."

His jaw clenched. Mine did too. So did my fists and every other muscle in my body.

Jerry touched my arm. He could see the tension I was carrying. Another deep breath. "I kept asking myself, Byron—why were Becca and Erin chosen out of all the girls in Vegas?"

He shrugged. "It's that age, you know. Those perverts go after the girls who are young, cute, and easy to manipulate. I just hope they catch the bastards who did this to the girls. To you, Alex. To Sonya and me. It's got to stop."

I nodded. "Oh yeah, it's going to stop. Right fucking now."

He looked like he'd just had a rotten egg shoved up his nose.

"You're right about the perverts, Byron. I've seen them, smelled them even. They're worse than you can possibly imagine. And they drugged your daughter. They beat your daughter. And they raped your daughter." I could feel tears welling in my eyes—fueled by sadness and rage—for what Becca had experienced, for what Erin had experienced.

Byron looked at the pool, scratching his chin. His hand had the jitters. A chemical reaction, or were the words finally evoking true emotion?

"You know Dmitri, don't you, Byron?"

"I don't know what you're talking about." He had no

conviction behind his words. It almost sounded robotic. He kept his gaze on the pool.

"You're a druggie, Byron. You, like so many others, are addicted to fentanyl, aren't you?"

He didn't move for a second. Then, he pulled his knees up and put his hands over his ears, as if he couldn't bear to hear any more.

I gave him a moment.

"I didn't want to do it," he said, his voice cracking. "But that Russian fuck wouldn't drop it. He wouldn't cut me a break or give me more time to pay back the debt. He didn't care about anyone except himself."

Miraculously, I held back a nasty retort. Instead, I asked, "How did it go down, Byron?"

He closed his eyes. His skin turned ruddy. "I ran into Dmitri at a party here in Vegas about a year ago. He was suave, European, had women draping all over him. I was a little envious. He said he could hook me up."

He swallowed. "From the very first pill he gave me, it took me to a place I'd never felt. All the booze I'd downed over the years never came close to this feeling. I was on top of the world. Nothing could hurt me. After I came down from that high, I knew I had to experience it again. He showed up at my room the next day, almost like he knew I'd be begging him for more. He gave me more, but at a price. I had money, so it didn't matter much at first. Eventually, I got back home, tried to settle into my normal life…well, my normal life of being a walking, talking drunk. But it just wasn't enough."

He looked up with pleading eyes that were so bloodshot it was hard to see the white. I crossed my arms, didn't say a word.

"He supplied me the drugs, and I paid. But after a while, I needed so many just to get through a week, it was more than I made. We couldn't pay the mortgage or car payments. It got bad. We were saved by Sonya's parents one month, but I was desperate…for money, for the pills, for the escape of it all. I planned a trip out here for spring break and thought I'd talk to Dmitri in person and get it all worked out. But he didn't see it the same way. He got pissed and told me there was only one way he'd remove all the debt. I had to find someone competent to carry his drugs from LA back to Vegas. Taking the girls, though, was his idea."

"So it was all him, not you? Is that what you're telling me?"

He grabbed his head with both hands and shook and cried. After a few seconds, he got it under control. "You're right, Alex. I chose to ignore the danger the girls would be in. I had a feeling he was into some bad stuff, including using girls as prostitutes. I…I knew it, but I did it anyway."

"So," Jerry said, "you worked with Dmitri to set up those calls to your wife and Alex?"

He nodded. "I guess I hoped that Alex would come through and that the girls would be released in a few hours, and other than a little bit of a scare, we'd all be fine. No harm, no foul, right?"

Sonya walked over and grabbed a towel. "Alex…Byron? What's going on?"

I spotted Becca, who was smiling in the pool, talking to another girl her age. And then I looked at Sonya. "I'm sorry for you. I'm sorry for your family."

Jerry put his hand on my shoulder. "I'll take it from here, Alex. You've got business to attend to."

I patted his arm and walked off with tears raining down my face.

Thirty-Nine

Ivy

In my tenure at CPS, and even during my time in running ECHO, I rarely had the chance to reunite a child with her parent when neither was at fault for any wrongdoing.

But right now was one of those few precious moments. Along with Cristina and the FBI agent in the back seat, I pulled up to the curb in front of the Bailey home. Before the car had rocked to a stop, Angel had thrown open the door and jumped out.

"Careful now," the agent said.

I shifted the gear to park and watched Angel run into her father's arms. Gerald picked her up, spun her around. A moment later, little Lila poked her head out the front door of the house. With a toothy smile on her face, she barreled into her father and sister.

We gave them all the time they needed. Eventually, Lila ran back inside. I took that as my cue to walk up the sidewalk and speak to Gerald. With his arm still wrapped around Angel, he reached out and grabbed my hand. Tears of joy ran down his face.

"Thank you. You have no idea the gift you've given me."

I smiled. We talked for a couple of minutes and Angel learned that her mother was in a detox center.

"I hope she feels better, and we can become a family again," Angel said.

"I hope so too, sweetie," her father said, giving her a kiss on the forehead. "Just know it's going to be a long road. She's going to need to see a counselor, and I'll probably join her."

"I'll go too. Anything for Mom," she said, wiping a tear from her cheek.

I was amazed at her ability to not hold a grudge against her mother. I didn't want to mention that her mother might face criminal charges. Now was a time for healing and forgiveness—two things kids rarely see from their parents, at least in my experience.

I gave Angel a final hug and said goodbye.

As I got back into the car, I received a text from Saul. We'd been going back and forth since I'd bought a phone at the airport.

"Are you and Saul sexting again?" Cristina asked.

I looked at the agent in the back seat. She half-smiled and went back to reading something on her phone.

"We're not sexting."

"Okay, doing your *xoxo* thing. You're just so giddy these days, like a love-struck teenager or something."

"What can I say? We're—"

"In love. Right. Got it." She gave me the thumbs-up. "Did I tell you that Brice asked me out?'

"Uh, no. What happened to Poppy?"

"We realized we were just friends. But Brice is…hot." She smiled.

I nodded.

She smacked her hands against her jeans "So, are you ready to dive into teacher background checks?"

"Almost."

"Almost," she repeated, as if she were in deep thought. "Wait, you said something about meeting your friend, Alex, in Austin. Is that now?" she asked, pointing downward.

I nodded.

"Why would you do that when you just got back from almost being killed by those Russian amigos?"

"It's something I really need to do."

"Can't Alex do it on her own?"

"Maybe. But something is pulling me. I can't explain it. It's bigger than me, bigger than Alex."

She shrugged. "I guess I can knock out a few while you're gone."

After dropping off the agent at the airport and Cristina at her apartment, I jumped on I-35 and drove north to Austin. In a couple of hours, two more lives would forever be changed. And I knew I had to be there for my friends.

Forty

Alex

Ivy and I stood at the side of my rental car just off the curb of a street in old west Austin. The street was lined with lush trees and homes as unique as the city, long known for embracing its "weirdness." It had taken longer than expected to hunt down Ozzie. We had first dropped by his apartment. He didn't answer the door, but a neighbor of his, a nice gentleman named Ervin, had steered us to this home—the old house that he and Nicole had purchased only weeks before he saw the love of his life plunge to her death.

Or so he'd thought.

My eyes glanced at the yellow and brown *For Sale* sign in the front yard, then I lifted my sights and saw Nicole Novak—a.k.a. Liv Bradshaw—walk the last few steps toward the front door. Her gait was apprehensive, almost like a young flower girl ambling up the aisle in a church wedding. But I knew she was bursting with excitement. Of course, this excitement had only come after a period of great mourning and grief.

I thought back to what had transpired in the last twenty-four hours, starting with the news that would, for the second time in the last few months, alter the paths of more than one life. In the screened-in porch of Bruce Massey's in-laws' home, Holt told Nicole that her parents had been murdered in Belgium through some type of nerve agent that had touched their skin in a crowded train station. At first, Nicole was quiet, as if all her emotion had been sucked out of her long ago. But slowly, over a few minutes, she began to cry. Ivy and I did our best to console her.

"For years, I wasn't even sure they were alive. And now that they're actually dead...I don't know. It's just so unfair."

That night, since I only had minutes before heading off to join the raid on Dmitri's compound, Ivy and I learned part of the story. Unbeknownst to anyone, including Ozzie, Nicole's parents had worked as double agents, infiltrating the GRU—Russia's foreign intelligence agency—while actually working for the CIA. It had taken the couple years to slowly work their way into a position where they would provide useful information back to the CIA. But they were outed by someone who held a grudge against the CIA and narrowly escaped their first encounter with Russian agents who'd hunted them down just outside of Moscow. While they were on the run, the CIA believed that the Russians had learned of the Ramseys' one and only offspring, and that was when Nicole had also become a potential target. She had to go into hiding to protect anyone who might also be a target because of knowing her—such as Ozzie and his daughter, Mackenzie.

"Nicole is so nervous," Ivy said, bringing me back to the present scene. "I know she doesn't want to give Ozzie a heart attack."

"But she wanted to do it in person," I said. "She thought that if she called him, he wouldn't believe her—and not just because he can't hear very well. She was really concerned he would think it was a very cruel joke."

Nicole brought her hand up to the door, paused, and then

rapped three times.

Everyone thought I was this hero for rushing into dangerous situations to help people I cared about. But could I actually walk away from the people I loved most to keep them safe, fake my own death, knowing that I'd probably never see them again? That was what Nicole had done. It was the ultimate act of love...where the recipient may never know the truth.

Nicole had waited until we met up with Ivy an hour earlier to share the first part of her story. She said she first learned of her parents' danger when FBI agents snuck a note into her purse while she was attending a marketing conference in New York. She'd met an agent at a bar, and he'd explained everything. At first, she was in shock, simply because she hadn't heard from her parents in years. She wondered if they'd died while serving the country they loved. After she took in that new information, the agent brought in Holt, and he gave her the options. She only had one day to get back to him, so they could plan her exit strategy. She didn't sleep a wink and was tormented every minute of those twenty-four hours.

In the end, she made the call to fake her own death. At first, they weren't sure how it would go down—until the FBI learned of the obsession of one of her old college friends, Mitch Durant. She'd turned down his advances at the conference. At the time, she didn't think it was more than a guy having too much to drink. Then, the FBI started digging into Mitch's life. What they found was a very deranged person, and someone who had more than an infatuation with Nicole. As they monitored his communication, they learned he'd hired a known hitman, Bruno Hopper, to kill Nicole. This, Holt had told her, would be the catalyst for making this event so believable that no one would question it. And that would allow them to achieve their goal—protect Ozzie and Mackenzie, while Nicole would start a new life after undergoing some changes to her appearance.

Holt and a few agents in the FBI Witness Protection Program worked behind the scenes to make it all happen. They found out when Hopper was in Austin. They tracked his whereabouts and his communication to Durant. They had a stuntwoman on the ready. She'd altered her appearance to look similar to Nicole. Nicole knew she could get word from Holt and his team at any moment. It just happened to be when she was leaving work to meet Ozzie to celebrate their anniversary. She was near the bridge that day, but not on it, talking to Ozzie on the phone, pulling off the act like a seasoned actor. The stuntwoman wore a Kevlar vest, took three bullets to her chest, and fell off the bridge. She lived—agents helped her out of the raging river minutes after she'd dropped in.

I asked Nicole about the ring finger—police had found a severed finger with her rings on it in the river—since I noticed she had all ten of her fingers. She said the finger was from a cadaver. She had to give up her rings anyway, so this was one way she knew Ozzie would be able to keep her rings.

After hearing the full story, Ivy and I were stunned into silence for more than a few minutes.

"Ozzie had no idea your parents were in the CIA?" Ivy asked.

"I couldn't tell him. When I left school at Cal-Berkley after we met, it was to go see them in Europe. I thought it might be my last time to ever see them."

After that, we hugged Nicole with everything we had. And then we began the final leg of her trip.

Back to the present scene. "Do you think Ozzie's even here?" Ivy asked. "Maybe he ran off to a hardware store, or to pick up Mackenzie from school."

A second later, the front door opened. Ozzie, all six-foot-three of him, just stood there in his blue and gold Cal-Berkley T-shirt. His mouth opened, but his lips didn't move. His gaze stayed on this woman with the snake tattoo. Nicole put her hands together as if she were in prayer. And then, as if some magical force were in control, they came together at the exact same time.

It hit me like a thunderclap—a shockwave of love had just exploded in front of me. They rocked left and right. I could hear both of them crying. Then they paused as he clutched her shoulders and shook his head.

"Is this when the questions start?" Ivy asked with a sniffle.

She draped her arm inside of mine, and I leaned into her. For some reason, I not only felt this kinship with Ozzie, but I was also happy to share this moment with Ivy. Tears drained down my face, and Ivy handed me a tissue.

"Thanks."

"I came prepared," she said through an emotion-filled giggle.

Just then, Ozzie looked up and saw us. He put his hand over his heart and shouted, "Thank you. Thank you for bringing back the love of my life. I love you guys!"

"Back at you," I yelled with a huge smile.

We watched them as they hugged and cried and kissed for the next ten minutes. It gave me hope that there was indeed more love in this world than hate.

Forty-One

Wearing a ball cap, yoga pants, a Lycra workout shirt, and sport sunglasses, the woman pulled on the leash of the three-year-old Australian shepherd. The little guy immediately stopped and sat on his hind legs. She leaned down and rubbed his ears. She'd only known him for a short while, but she had this sixth sense with dogs—some had even called her the Dog Whisperer.

Even though all dogs were as different as little children, she could understand what dogs wanted, appreciated. This Aussie dog—she wasn't sure of his name—was all about his ears. Rub those ears, and he'll be your friend for life.

She probably only needed that obedience for a couple of hours. She extended her leg and stretched her hamstring, then did the same on the other leg, all while watching the scene play out a block down the street.

Her gaze gravitated toward the lean woman standing at the curb. Not the younger woman, but the one who held her head up high, who had a noble grace about her, yet who carried herself with serious intent, as if she knew she was put on this earth to right all the wrongs…to be a spark of hope.

Alex Troutt was stunning and magnificent. Her features and piercing eyes would make your knees wobble. But it was how she'd overcome so many obstacles in her life that made her special. She had evolved into the kind of person who should be held up as the example for all young people, girls and boys alike.

The woman twisted her torso left and right—ensuring that she'd be viewed as just another Austinite out on her daily run with her dog. Every couple of seconds, her eyes couldn't help but shift back to Alex and the others—two women and a tall man, striking in his own way. They were all talking, laughing as a group.

She took in a deep breath. It had been quite a journey over the last week. Tracking a person without their knowledge with so much on the line had been difficult. She'd lost weight due to a lack of food, sleep, and yes, the stress. On more than one occasion, she thought she might lose Alex. In fact, she'd almost stepped in to lend a hand—which, to be truthful, had been one of her fantasies. But she'd withheld the urge and was ultimately rewarded by watching her hero win out once again.

Alex Troutt, in all her glory, had everything she desired.

The dog leaned against her leg—showing his trust in her—and then he looked up and wagged his tail. She smiled, rubbed his ears again. She took in another fortifying breath as she glanced at Alex again. She knew it was time to shift the paradigm and join the game. It was time for Alex to pursue her.

Her body tingled with delight. She couldn't wait to get started.

John W. Mefford Bibliography

The Alex Troutt Thrillers (Redemption Thriller Collection)
AT BAY (Book 1)
AT LARGE (Book 2)
AT ONCE (Book 3)
AT DAWN (Book 4)
AT DUSK (Book 5)
AT LAST (Book 6)
AT STAKE (Book 7)
AT ANY COST (Book 8)
BACK AT YOU (Book 9)
AT EVERY TURN (Book 10)
AT DEATH'S DOOR (Book 11)
AT FULL TILT (Book 12)

The Ivy Nash Thrillers (Redemption Thriller Collection)
IN DEFIANCE (Book 1)
IN PURSUIT (Book 2)
IN DOUBT (Book 3)
BREAK IN (Book 4)
IN CONTROL (Book 5)
IN THE END (Book 6)

The Ozzie Novak Thrillers (Redemption Thriller Collection)
ON EDGE (Book 1)

BACK AT YOU
GAME ON (Book 2)
ON THE ROCKS (Book 3)
SHAME ON YOU (Book 4)
ON FIRE (Book 5)
ON THE RUN (Book 6)

The Ball & Chain Thrillers
MERCY (Book 1)
FEAR (Book 2)
BURY (Book 3)
LURE (Book 4)
PREY (Book 5)
VANISH (Book 6)
ESCAPE (Book 7)
TRAP (Book 8)

The Booker Thrillers
BOOKER – Streets of Mayhem (Book 1)
BOOKER – Tap That (Book 2)
BOOKER – Hate City (Book 3)
BOOKER – Blood Ring (Book 4)
BOOKER – No Más (Book 5)
BOOKER – Dead Heat (Book 6)

The Greed Thrillers
FATAL GREED (Book 1)
LETHAL GREED (Book 2)
WICKED GREED (Book 3)
GREED MANIFESTO (Book 4)

To stay updated on John's latest releases, visit:
JohnWMefford.com

Made in United States
Cleveland, OH
14 April 2025